'Remarkably imaginative and lyrical ... **highly original**.'
Daily Mail

'**A joy to read**.'
Carousel

'**Fish food for the soul**.'
The Times

'Distinctive ... moving, funny. **This is the real thing**.'
David Almond, author of *Skellig*

'A **terrifically talented** writer ... strange and beguiling,
quirky and literary ... her assured debut
captured my heart.'
Bookseller

'A book apart ... **Literary prizes this way please**.'
Observer

'**Rare and remarkable**.'
The Sunday Times

'**Beautifully written**.'
Irish Independent

'**Grips you from the start**.'
BookTrust

'**Superb**. Original, heart warming, shocking and magical.'
Emma Carroll, author of *Letters from the Lighthouse*

'Magical, mysterious, utterly charming.'
Book Bag

'A debut novel to savour.'
Julia Eccleshare, Lovereading4kids

'A beautiful piece of fiction.'
Countryfile

'Unforgettable.' ★★★★★
Books for Keeps

'Funny, sad, poignant, quirky and unique.'
Katie, age 12, Lovereading4kids

'Distinctive and authentic from the first page.'
Irish Times

'Full of **adventure**, friendship and love. Has you **hooked**
from the first page.'
Isaac, age 10, Lovereading4kids

'Utterly unusual and mesmerising.'
Abi Elphinstone, author of *Sky Song*

'An astonishing tale, truly special!'
Cally, age 10, Lovereading4kids

'It's **terrific**. The workings of a creatively acrobatic mind.'
Brian Conaghan, author of *We Come Apart*

'Sparkling and unique.'
Minerva Reads

The Boy Who Hit Play

ABOUT THE AUTHOR

Fish Boy was Chloe Daykin's first novel, which she wrote while studying for her MA in Creative Writing at Newcastle University. It won a Northern Writers' Award, was nominated for the CILIP Carnegie Medal, longlisted for the UKLA Book Awards, shortlisted for the Branford Boase and garnered critical acclaim. An artist, designer, playwright and teacher, Chloe is always up for an unusual adventure and lives in Northumberland with her family. *The Boy Who Hit Play* is her second novel.

BY THE SAME AUTHOR

Fish Boy

The Boy Who Hit Play

Chloe Daykin

FABER & FABER

First published in 2018
by Faber & Faber Limited
Bloomsbury House
74–77 Great Russell Street
London, WC1B 3DA

Typeset by Faber
Printed by CPI Group (UK) Ltd, Croydon CR0 4YY
All rights reserved
Text © Chloe Daykin, 2018

A CIP record for this book is available
from the British Library

ISBN 978–0–571–32678–5

FSC
www.fsc.org
MIX
Paper from
responsible sources
FSC® C020471

2 4 6 8 10 9 7 5 3 1

For everyone I love
without whom I'd be
sunk, many, many times.

Prologue

What if it is the 25th of June 2005 and it's sunny, and in Brymont on Sea, down Minton Street, opposite the Happy Shopper there is a zoo? And what if in that zoo there is a man in a large hat? What if the man looks at the screech owls, walks past the monkeys, slips a lost hedgehog into his pocket and is about to sit on a bench? But stops.

Because there is a newspaper on this bench. A wriggly one.

What if this man lifts up the paper and underneath is a baby and on the front of the wriggly baby's vest is a message in big black letters that says:

HELP

And what if the hedgehog-pocketing, owl-watching man picks the baby up and puts it in his hat and walks away quietly, 'cos that is his style, 'cos he has a Stetson which is nice and roomy and just the right size for a baby, 'cos he is a doing a country-and-western gig in aid of the hospice and he is excellent, 'cos he is George Arthur Lucas and that baby is me and this is how I begin.

Pause

Into a space that is blank and buzzy and alive with possibilities, with expectation, the kind of space where anything can happen
    the space to crawl
        to walk
           to talk
              to grow
                  to live
                      to become
                          someone
                          me
                              Elvis
                                  Crampton
                                  Lucas.

Hello.

Hi.

Yes you.

Howdy.

I am Elvis Crampton Lucas, soundsmith and YouTuber. Welcome to my world.

Elvis

Elvis Presley came from Tupelo, Mississippi.

He was great at dancing and singing and looking cool.

People thought he was the coolest.

He sold six hundred million records.

Won three Grammy awards.

By forty-two, he was very ugly and rich and unhappy.

And died on the toilet eating cheeseburgers.*

I am not that Elvis.

---

* kind of

Fast Forward

It is the 25th of June 2017. It is actually my discovery day but we call it my birthday because we don't know when my birthday is, because of the bench and the zoo and the newspaper. But we sing happy birthday, 'cos happy discovery day doesn't flow so well and I record this on my phone on top of the cupboard, 'cos sounds are better when they float.

Right now I am standing in front of the candles on my triple-decker Oreo chunk cake, which is on the plate with hand-drawn eyeballs on, which is on the tablecloth with hand-drawn song lyrics on, in front of the sofa with Aunty Ima, Lulu, Lloyd and Next-Door-Duncan on, with Dad's hand on my shoulder, the shoulder with my new home-knit birthday jumper from Aunty Ima on, when it happens.

Aunty Ima, Dad, Duncan and Lloyd have finished singing happy birthday (but not Lulu as she is a cat and can only yowl) and are clapping and saying, 'Make a wish, make a wish,' and

Next-Door-Duncan is saying, 'Make a with,' because of his braces, and Dad pulls something out of his pocket and says, 'This is for you.' He hands it over. It's smooth and round. I click the top and look down into the swinging needle of a compass. 'It was my dad's and his dad's and his,' he says. 'It's a father-son thing.'

'OK.'

I think about the bench.

I think about Dad's dad and his dad and his.

And a thought bubbles out of my body and into my brain before I can stop it. I try to keep it in. I do try. But it is too quick and the wish is on my tongue and out.

'I wish I knew *why?*' I say, and everything stops.

Freeze

Like music where the drumbeats go on beating but
time stops ticking and you're waiting for the rhythm
to kick in, to beef itself back up, for everything to
start. The drums drum and the bass is thumping
and you're waiting and I'm waiting and . . .

I can't believe I wished it but I have

and I try and make a new wish up
but it is no good, it's just too
   late.

Everyone has gone quiet. Lulu jumps off the sofa
and goes into the kitchen. Lloyd puts his hands over
his ears. Dad is staring out of the window. Aunty
Ima serves out some cake slices. And even though
the triple-decker Oreo-chunk cake is delicious,
all I'm tasting is guilt and worry and a feeling
of weirdness.

A Name

Twelve years ago, George Lucas took me home off the bench and put his hand to his vinyl collection. He picked out the first three albums his fingers came to and named me after them.

Elvis Presley – by Elvis Presley
The Cramps – *A Date with Elvis*
Tonight – David Bowie

Elvis
Cramp
Ton
Lucas after George Arthur Lucas.
Sometimes I wonder what it would be like to be
Thomas
or
Christopher
or
James.

But I am not.

Sometimes I wonder if names are like clothes that someone else has picked.

Do you grow into them?

Or do they never really fit?

George Lucas

George Lucas is my dad. Not *that* George Lucas, not the *Star Wars/Indiana Jones* one, not the one with the Skywalker Ranch in Nicasio, California. George Lucas in a three-storey terrace on Brymont on Sea, with a basement full of rescued hedgehogs and a large collection of fridge magnets. The baby-in-a-Stetson George Lucas, with a moustache like a goalpost and froth hair. George Lucas, musician and NHS call-centre worker on the side. Times are hard for musicians. I think maybe they're always hard.

I love George Lucas, even though he plays 'Blue Moon' on his trumpet in the evenings and shreds my mini Weetabix boxes and toilet-roll collection for the hedgehog bedding. He is the best George Lucas anyone could ever have. He has been my George Lucas for as long as I know. Forever.

Right now, he's sitting on my bed, on the Arsenal duvet. I don't support Arsenal. Or like football. It's a present from Aunty Ima. Sometimes her taste is a bit

off.

But I don't say it.

I've burst the balloons.

Everyone's gone home.

It's just us.

We cut the silence with our night time 'guess that tune' game.

Dad pulls some castanets out of his jeans. He always wears jeans. He calls it his home uniform. It's kind of his work one too. He diagnoses illnesses behind plastic call-centre screens, so technically, he says, he could be wearing boxers. No one would know.

He clacks tunes out and I guess.

'"Funky Town".'

'Yes.'

'"I Want to Break Free" . . .'

'Yes.' Dad's castanets stop mid clack.

'Thanks for this, Dad,' I say, and hold up the compass.

'It was what your grandad would have wanted.'

'I thought Grandad was a carpet fitter?' I flip it open.

'He was. His dad's dad's dad's dad was a sailor.'

'OK.' I look at the dials. 'Dad.'

'Yeah.'

'It's time, isn't it?' I say. 'For . . .

It.

         Me.

   You.

           Us.

        The bench.

   The zoo.

            The question.

     Why?'

I look up. 'Who put me there? It's time to find the answer.'

'You know, Elvis –' he shuffles up the bed on to the Gunners' gun – 'of all the things that can pop out of a hat . . .' he says.

'Rabbits?' I say.

'Mice?'

'Doves?'

'Budgies?' he says and we both shrug. 'I'm glad it was you.'

'Of all the people who could have picked me up

12

and put me in a hat . . .' I put the castanets on Arsene Wenger's eyes.

'That's probably not many,' he says. 'It's hard to get a good Stetson these days.'

'I'm glad it was you.'

'Me too,' he says and ruffles my hair.

'Team on?' I say and tap his knuckles.

'Team on,' he says and taps back.

'With Lloyd Partington!' And Lloyd, Dad's best-friend-apple-buff-and-window-cleaner Partington, climbs in through the window with two Braeburns bulging in the pockets of his holey tracksuit bottoms and and attacks Dad with a blown-up paper bag for an added element of surprise.

BANG.

Dad bursts the bag.

It lies on the floor.

And we salute one another because this is how things are done and this is how it all begins.

Thinking Is All

Dad goes downstairs and Lloyd goes back out the window.

I switch on my detective brain.

Detective work is really a matter of making a list and crossing everything off it till you're left with the answer. But first, to get to the list you must ask lots of questions and this requires thinking.

Thinking is the difference between darkness and discovery.

Thinking

is

all.

Sherlock Holmes smokes a pipe. Scooby and Shaggy eat Scooby Snacks while Thelma works it out. I make music. It's the way my brain is wired. Before I could talk, I sang. Music moves through me, comes alive in my blood. I am a collector of sounds, my iPhone recorder by my side. Sounds soothe my soul – when I listen I'm somewhere else. Tuned out.

I scratch out a samba with a biro and think.

Rewind.

To the zoo.

To me. On a bench.

Just a wriggly baby. Not going wah wah wah, but sleeping and possibly weeing itself 'cos that's what babies do, right?

If you have a problem with zoos and think it's very cruel, you don't need to worry 'cos it isn't that sort of a zoo. But if you like, you could imagine a safari park or a nature reserve. But that's not where it was. It was a zoo. And if you have a problem with newspapers you can imagine a box of tissues or a magazine or a tea towel. But it wasn't in a safari park with a tea towel. It was at a zoo with a newspaper.

List 1: What kind of people go to zoos?

List 2: What kind of people have babies?

List 3: What kind of people read newspapers?

What kind of people leave babies?

What kind of person left me?

Why?

KNOCK, KNOCK.

'Who's there?'

'Cocoa calling.'

It's Aunty Ima.

Aunty Ima moved in last year to help out with the rent. Food and knitting are her best things. She sells her stuff on Etsy in a shop called Once a Knitter Never a Quitter. I wonder how many pineapple tea cosies it took to buy my phone last year.

She pours hot chocolate from a pan into the red reindeer mug. It is thick and dark and delicious. We sit together not saying anything and I click my phone and record:

> *silence thoughtful*
> *(a hissy fuzzy, rain-on-the-window,*
> *fly-in-the-lampshade sound).*

'The past is a strange place,' she says, 'but sometimes it's a place you need to visit.'

Skip

This is where it started.

The train, the plane, the gun, the boat and the rest of my life.

If life was like iPods, I could've fast-forwarded to see it.

But it isn't.

And I couldn't.

Would I change it?

No.

I wouldn't change a single minute.

This is that story.

This is how I'm here.

On this jetty.

Face to face with the future.

See you in sixteen days.

OK?

Remember the newspaper.

The title on it says:

Aftenposten

It isn't from round here.

It's from the land of snow and ice and mountains like forever.

I go downstairs in my pyjamas. Dad is feeding the hedgehogs in the basement. The walls are lined with wooden walkways and leaf piles and earth and hedgehog houses that look like wicker igloos.

'Hey, Dad.'

'Hey.' He looks up. 'Nice pyjamas.'

'Cheers.' They're Christmas-tree ones. From Aunty Ima. He holds out the bag of Spikes Semi-moist nibbles and we put handfuls of it into the little metal trays. A hedgehog unrolls and waddles over and starts crunching.

I hold the paper up. 'We have to go here.'

'I wish we could, son.' Dad whistles. 'But . . .'

'What?' I pick up a hedgehog. It snuggles into my elbow.

'It's the most expensive place on earth.'

'I could sell my Lego.' My hedgehog rubs its nose up my sleeve.

Lloyd climbs in through the basement window. Our windows are like cat flaps for Lloyd. He comes when he wants. It's always been like that. Dad says Lloyd just turned up in his life like a hedgehog.

Lloyd dusts off his knees. 'I'm paying,' he says.

'How?' Dad clips the nibbles shut.

'I'll find a way.' Lloyd bows his head. 'It's the least I can do.'

'Nice!' I high-five Lloyd. We've never been on holiday. We've never been anywhere. Call-centre wages are tricky and not very stretchy. The hedgehog grips.

'George.' Lloyd takes a deep breath. 'Can we discuss matters?' He looks at me. 'In private.'

I go outside and listen by the door.

Dad opens it. 'See you up in a minute,' he says.

I go upstairs.

Dad and Lloyd discuss matters for *ages* and Dad comes up looking weird.

'Elvis.' His voice is squeaky. 'Have you had a happy life?'

I think back over everything. 'Yeah,' I say. 'It's been the best.'

'Good.' He nods and looks like he's going to be sick or cry or hit someone. 'We're going,' he says. 'We're definitely definitely going.' And hugs me and shuts the door.

Weird.

Unlocking

We make plans.

1 – My plan is the *Aftenposten*.

2 – Lloyd's plan is money.

3 – Dad's plan is suitcases and passports and Jet2.

When Dad clicks on 'BUY NOW', I think about the money floating through the air out of the account and get this wobbly deep-down feeling.

When I was a kid I used to think my parents were spies on a mission, at risk of death. Now I just don't know. I have no photos or memories or anything.

I have bits of me that might be like them.

But I don't know.

I have no way of knowing.

When I think about them it's like music I can't quite hear. Like I'm walking past a door and there's sound coming out but it's shut. And they're on the other side.

I wanna open it.

But what if it's a door that doesn't wanna be opened?

What if you can't open a door with a newspaper?

Dad looks at me. His eyes are red and puffy. 'You OK?'

I swallow the wobble. 'Sure.' I nod. 'You?'

'Hmmn.' He strokes his chin.

Actually I hate flying. Well I've never flown. I hate the idea of it. I wish we could teleport. I watch the little red plane giff taking off and lean over and click the screen on to *Top 10 Ways to Survive a Plane Crash*.

YouTube is the soundtrack to my life.

We take ID photos of ourselves at Tesco's and wait for the summer holidays to come round and school to end and the passports to turn up.

I can't believe we're actually leaving Brymont. If Brymont had a soundtrack it'd be slow and grey. The sound of lorries in snow mush. TripAdvisor gives Brymont two and half stars. I think that's fair.

I sit on my bed and click on to YouTube out into the world.

I started uploading my own stuff last year.

I do music with images. Weird stuff. My things.

I have eighty-one subscribers.

I look at the screen.

My video has a hundred and thirty-eight likes.

Cool.

The looking and checking is kind of addictive.

JaxOpossum says:

I like this. Kind of reminds me of the Orb in the early days.

FelixOpacha says:

Had this stuck in my head all day. 😃

CokeCan says:

I LOVE this. 😜

StickitSquirrel says:

This sucks. 👎

I switch it off.

Lloyd comes over and we look at maps and travel brochures.

I look at the prices and think about Lloyd's plan. Money. *I'll find a way.*

'Did you find a way?' We bunch up on the sofa.

Lloyd nods and taps his nose.

I look at waterfalls and wolves and forest mists.

Dad looks at ships sailing past skies and purple mountains off into nowhere.

Lloyd looks at naked people in canoes and shuts the magazine.

And in five days' time Dad's eyes unpuff and he brings a big black suitcase into my room and unclicks the lock.

Ready?

Dad unzips the lid and Lloyd jumps out eating a Royal Gala.

I get my phone and record:

apple-eating excitement
(an apple-eating, draw-opening,
'out of the way please' kind of sound).

I pull open a draw. We stare at my mess of socks and pants. 'What do we need?'

'Things of the world,' he says.

'Hot things?' I think about the naked canoeists. We scoop up all of my pants.

'Cold things?' I think of snow and killer whales and ice lakes.

We scoop up all of my socks. 'The key to packing is preparation,' he says. 'And layering. You never know what life's going to throw at you. But generally, if you can layer up, it hurts less. Or at least it's less of a surprise.' He looks at Lloyd and pulls his jumper up to show his Wolverine T-shirt underneath. It is a surprise.

Lloyd looks at his socks and says, 'Every apple needs its skin.'

I think of skinless apples. The fruit inside that would be knackered without it. I wonder how thick our skin is to stop us from spilling out. I pick up a jumper.

'Wear your heavy stuff,' Dad says. 'It saves on the baggage allowance.'

Lloyd jumps out from hiding under the duvet and says, 'surprise!' and we stick everything in and pull the lid over. Lloyd has to lie across it like a starfish to spread his weight while I pull the zip round from one end. Dad takes the other end. I get a bit stuck going past Lloyd's knees.

'OW!'

It is a shame he is wearing shorts.

Our zips meet in the middle. Lloyd wipes the blood off his knee and gets his fish-weighing hook out of his Asda 'bag for life' and we weigh it.

It is forty-seven grams over the limit. I take out the snorkel set.

We're ready.

'Three thousand, six hundred and twenty-eight grammes.' Lloyd weighs his arms with the case weigher.

Dad pushes the case out the door. Lloyd takes my HELP Babygro out of my special-things box and shakes it like he expects something to fall out.

It doesn't.

'It's just a Babygro, Lloyd.' I take it back.

'Just looking for clues,' he says.

I put it away in the special box and take my birth newspaper out. I check it over like I've checked it a million times. When I was little I was sure there'd be dots under the letters to make code, to make a message. There aren't.

I put it in my rucksack.

And wake up to the Skoda Starline taxi.

Go

Three cases stand by the door.

Mine. Dad's. Lloyd's.

Aunty Ima isn't coming. 'Someone has to look after the hedgehogs,' she says and pulls one out of a tea cosy.

'Where's Lloyd?'

Dad knocks on the cupboard under the stairs. Lloyd comes out with a pillow and a blanket and wraps two pancakes in kitchen roll and puts them in his pocket. 'For the journey,' he says.

We hug Aunty Ima and get into the taxi, and out at the airport.

The driver gets the cases and squints in the sunshine and says, 'Nice for some, eh.'

Lloyd says, 'Life is nice for everyone who is able to love the world,' and pays.

We click through the automatic slidey doors. Lloyd disagrees with the grammage on the self-weigh bag-drop check-in and tries to fight it out with the machine, but Dad says it isn't worth it and we walk off before the assistant comes over.

Top 10 Ways to Survive a Plane Crash says to sit at the back where you are statistically less likely to die. And you have ninety seconds to leave the aircraft before it explodes.

'Dad.'

'Yeah.'

'Where are we sitting?'

'I dunno,' he says, and we follow the signs to security.

Lloyd has to empty out his Granny Smiths from his pockets but they are returned. His Not-In-My-Name anti-war badge isn't. Dad's penknife isn't either. They take my compass but pass it back after the metal detector. I put it in my secret inside pocket to keep it close.

We follow the glittery black path to duty-free. Lloyd takes his travel pouch out on a string from under his T-shirt and pulls out a wedge of cash.

'Where did you get that from?' Dad points at the wedge.

'Tesco.' He lifts the travel pouch.

'The cash.'

29

'I sold the family Winchester.'

'It's a rifle, Dad.' I shrug. Lloyd is a pacifist so it figures.

He hands us each ten pounds. 'Buy something extravagant,' he says.

I buy a supersize tin of Oreos that looks like a giant Oreo and feels pretty extravagant. I look at Dad. 'What're you getting?'

Dad tries all the whisky samples on the bar.

The man behind it stares at us. Dad says, 'What've you got for a tenner?'

And he says, '*Blends* are down there, sir.' And points. We find one.

Lloyd gets a caramel mocha – we all sit in Caffè Nero passing the cup around and dipping in miniature Oreos from my tin.

Lloyd takes a handful and says, 'Cheers.'

'Technically they're yours anyway.'

'A gift is a gift,' he says and winks, and then shouts, 'DUCK,' and pulls us under the table. A rubber bullet of a bouncy ball just misses his eye and smacks into the mocha. I look up and see a tweed-suit sleeve pull back behind a pillar. Weird.

'What was that?'

'Nothing.' Lloyd looks away.

I crawl out and pick the ball up off the floor. It's see-through with blue writing that says:

vote for experience!
protect your family, your property & yourself!

I put it in my pocket, and record:

Strange thing number one
(a kids-fighting-over-an-iPad, shoe-stepping,
trouser shuffling, 'you missed a bit' kind of sound).

Lloyd wipes his trousers.
And we go off to departure gate twenty-two.

Up

Why would someone do that to Lloyd?

Maybe it was a mistake?

Bouncy balls are pretty bouncy. I got one at Christmas once and broke Aunty Ima's china yak.

Maybe it was a joke? At school, year eights stick rosehips down each other's shirts to make it itch. I think about jokes that aren't funny.

'Look at everyone, Elvis,' Lloyd says. He looks round like a cat in a shopping centre.

The stewardess scans our boarding cards.

Elvis Crampton MSTR

George Lucas MR

Lloyd Rupert Raptar Partington SIR

'Nice to have you on board, Mr Lucas.' She hums the *Star Wars* tune and Dad smiles. She smiles back.

We walk on to the tarmac and up the steps.

I hand the steward my boarding card and he says, 'First row at the back.'

Forty per cent less chance of death.

Result.

I sit by the window. This is my first flight and I want to look out. If the engine's on fire I want to know about it. Lloyd isn't next to us. He's further up. Next to the emergency exit. He stands and mimes jumping out. The stewardess stares at him. He sits down.

I look at the diagrams on the back of the seat in front and remember not to crawl on the floor if there's a fire or I'll get squashed. A man with no hair next to Dad says, 'Unnatural isn't it. Flying.'

I look in my bag for my headphones and find a bunch of postcards and pens with a note:

Draw me what you see.
Aunty Ima XX

I pick out a red Sharpie and write:

I am on the plane.
I am squashed.

33

And draw a picture of a cloud opening up the plane with a tin opener and everyone falling out and going:

Aaaaaghh.

The plane rolls off, and the engines start. We blast forwards, the ground speeds, the air pushes my head back, and we go up.

We go up like riding a bike, like the air has plucked us off the earth.

My stomach leaps out the bottom of the plane. It is waving from the tarmac.

I look down.

Everything pulls away into squares of green and brown and grey and blue.

We don't fall out and die.

I look down at everything fitting into boxes.

Like a jigsaw.

With all the bits.

And I think, that'll be me soon.

That'll be me with all my missing pieces slotted in.

Won't it?

And we go higher and higher
till
    we
        are
            up
                over the clouds
                    and everything is white.

Downer

I click on my phone and look at the Wikipedia page I searched up before we got here.

Aftenposten ('The Evening Post') is the largest printed newspaper . . .

There's a photo. The office looks bright and new. And BIG.

When I was five we went to pick out a cake at Simeon's. I wanted the big one. With marzipan and chocolate writing and white iced flowers. We didn't have the money but Dad bought it anyway and when we got home I took one bite and spat it out. It had rum cream in. I didn't know it had rum cream in.

I remember scraping the plate into the bin.

And Dad's face. 'It's OK, it's OK, we didn't know.' His hand on my back.

I remember that taste.

DISAPPOINTMENT.

I don't want to be disappointing.

I pick my fingers. 'Dad.'

The steward hands us two lasagnes on red trays. Dad tries to hand them back.

'Courtesy of the man with the holey trousers, sir,' he says and points to Lloyd who is waving his plastic cutlery at us.

The man with no hair nudges Dad. 'Hope it isn't full of horse meat, eh,' he says and eats his homemade cheese sandwich out of a lunch box. His crisp bag has swollen up like a balloon.

I take the plastic lid off the lasagne and steam bursts out. Dad aims the overhead ceiling fan at it on cold at full force. It makes my hair bounce. I poke at it with a fork and hope it doesn't contain horse. I wonder why horses are worse than cows? Or pigs? All animals deserve to live, don't they?

I sit and I wait until it's edible and won't melt my mouth skin, and I count the number of seat-belt signs I can see until the captain switches them off.

BING BONG.

I look at heads instead.

I see three bald ones and one hat and a plastic knife that chucks itself out of a seat and on to Lloyd who grabs it out of the air.

Strange thing number two.

37

I stand up.

'What are you doing?' Dad stares at me.

'Looking.' I look out for other weird things but see none and sit down.

I like the up. The up is OK.

We're not sucked out the windows into the sea.

I eat the lasagne and the steward takes the tray back. The plane tips. The engines buzz like wasps in bad moods.

We start to come down.

Out of the window is rocks. Massive ones coming up out of the sea. And the sea isn't blue, it's turquoise-green, and the rocks aren't grey, they're black. Giant lava-black rocks like claws with froth.

We go further over. The land is part land, part puddle. Green and water and water and green and mountains. No fields. No flat. Just islands and wetness. Land and sea pushing and pulling each other apart like drops of sun cream in a swimming pool. And islands. Small ones and big ones and ferries and boats and white-water trails and trees and cabins.

I put my headphones round my neck and chew.

'I trust a place with boats,' Dad says. 'It means people are open to adventure.'

'My favourite colour is green.' I put my hand to the window.

The green turns to concrete.

I look at the millions of people who must be down there.

'Dad.'

'It's all good, Elvis.'

Sometimes I think he's psychic. 'Is it?'

'You know what I did before we came here?' He doesn't wait for me to answer. 'I quit my job.' He smiles. 'I'm free.'

My inner lasagne turns to acid. I think of the basement: *It's the most expensive place on earth.* 'Why?'

'I hated my job.'

The wheels come out. The tarmac flashes under.

Dad hangs his head. 'They wouldn't give me the time off.'

We bang on to the ground.

He puts his arm round my shoulder. 'Welcome to Norway.'

Hamsters in Wheels

The seat-belt signs bing off. We walk down the steps and the sun is shining on the concrete.

'Won't you miss your job?'

'I'll miss my job like raw aubergine.'

'You hate that.'

'I know.'

'How will we survive?'

'I'll get a new one.' He soft-punches the wing. 'When we get back.'

We get on to a little bus that takes us to the terminal. There are no seats and we hold on to handles so we don't fall over. Two kids are playing thumb war and a girl keeps poking the window and saying, 'What's that, Mummy?'

'An aeroplane.'

'What's that, Mummy?'

'A bus.'

'What's that, Mummy?'

And the Dad says, 'That's a twin-engine multirole Typhoon.'

I think about Dad. I think of his face when he comes home from diagnosing colds and stomach bugs and shingles, sucking Strepsils 'cos people's ill voices make him feel ill.

Maybe he'll find something better?

The passport man smiles and says, 'Which one of you is Elvis?'

Dad and Lloyd say, 'Him,' and he sings 'Heartbreak Hotel' and nods and looks at our passports and lets us through.

Lloyd sits on the belt at the suitcase collection point and whirls round and round, and Dad pulls him off and gets our cases.

We drag them past two men on stools with credit-card leaflets and on into automatic spinning doors, which you have to time carefully, and out.

We take the suitcases through a car park and over the road, where we stand and look around and Lloyd spreads his arms and says, 'Behold.'

Then we wheel the cases all the way back in again and buy some hot dogs wrapped in bacon and wait for the *Flybussen*.

41

The sausages have hot-cheese middles. They are delicious. Lloyd bites off both ends and some hot cheese squirts out and runs down his T-shirt. Sometimes I wonder what having a brother would be like. Sometimes I think it's like Lloyd.

I draw Aunty Ima a postcard of a hot dog and a piece of cheese holding hands. On the back I write, 'Hot dogs and cheese are friends. Who knew?'

We lick our fingers clean.

The bus is slick and glidey.

It has different compartments underneath for different places. Me and Dad put our bags in the one for Oslo. Lloyd refuses to put his in.

He gets on and drags it up the steps with him.

The driver raises his arms and says, 'Tourists! Tourists!'

Lloyd raises his arms and says, 'Bus drivers! Bus drivers!'

Dad puts Lloyd's arms down and says, 'Let's get the tickets, eh,' and Lloyd takes loads of notes from his travel pouch. He doesn't get any change.

CLICK CLICK BRRRR RIP. We tear them off and sit down.

It is very high up on the bus.

42

I look at everyone and think, *you are Norwegians.*
I am amongst Norwegians. I wonder if I am one.
If I should feel at home.

A man says, 'Wow,' and takes a photo of a pigeon.

A Japanese family play I spy.

Lloyd sits on his case by the fold-down seats
opposite the middle doors. He always sits somewhere
different. Dad puts his trumpet on his knees and
looks at his phone.

BANG BANG BANG.

I jump.

Someone hits Lloyd's door.

A fist like a gun.

The bus drives off.

I turn and catch a blur of green tweed out the
back window.

There's no time to record:

> *strange thing number three*
> *(a head-twisting, what-the-f***-was-*
> *that (Dad) kind of sound).*

I push my head through the seats. 'Who was
that?'

43

'No one.' Lloyd says and shuts his eyes.

The bus driver drives on shouting at cars and braking lots.

'Does somebody not like you, Lloyd?'

'We are living in strange times,' he says and sticks his headphones on and starts shouting out Norwegian words:

Beklager

Nei

Mini Banker

People stare at him.

'I am learning new things,' he shouts.

The bus has free Wi-Fi which is great.

I check out YouTube.

A hundred and fifty-two likes.

Two hundred and twenty-one views. 👍

I watch videos of cats jumping out from behind sofas and attacking a woman in a onesie, and a hamster that falls asleep in its wheel, and they make me laugh.

I wonder how many other people in the world are laughing at these right now?

YouTube's like the magic hand of the universe.

Connecting everything.

I look out the window and watch the outside zooming by, which sometimes looks really normal and then really different, and feel a long way from everything and everyone we know.

I think about the mountains as big as volcanoes and cabins and waterways and boats.

They're here, they have to be here. Somewhere.

I know it.

Plan 1

The Surprise

Surprise!

We get off at the bus station and go out into a flow of people and cars and blue trams that are coming at us like caterpillars. We duck into a shop with cinnamon buns and sandwiches and bottles of Isklar.

A man in a black coat squashes backwards into a shelf of Cheez Doodles. 'After you,' he says and I squeeze through with my case.

Dad buys a hot chocolate and it is twenty krone. I don't know if this is a lot but I guess it is because we all share it. Dad has first go as he likes it hot as lava.

Lloyd goes last. When he has a drink I have the urge to smack the cup on the bottom, but I don't. It is a random brain flick of craziness which I control. Sometimes I think about things like that. I don't know if other people do.

Lloyd finishes the chocolate. I throw the cup under a truck to see if it squashes it. It does. It explodes. Dad walks into the road and picks it up and puts it in the compartmentalised recycling.

'Down!' Lloyd yells and ducks us down.

We drop on to the concrete.

TWANG.

A plastic crossbow arrow flies over our heads and into the O of the shop sign.

No one else seems to notice.

I see a man, a blur of green tweed, running away in the distance.

I look at Lloyd. 'Who *is* that?'

'Who?'

'HIM.' Me and Dad point at the green speck lost in the crowd.

'No one.'

We keep staring, not accepting his answer.

'That's Floyd Partington,' he says and looks down at his shoes.

'Who's that?'

'My brother. He was rather keen on the Winchester.' Lloyd unzips his suitcase. It turns out it is full of apples. Bags and bags of them, wrapped in newspaper. And two pairs of tracksuit bottoms. 'Apples are very expensive in Norway.' He strokes one and takes a bite. We stare at him. 'It's OK.' He lowers the apple. 'Floyd doesn't like water.'

'Why?'

'He got pushed in the moat once and nearly drowned.'

'In a moat?'

'It was at our house. We lived in a castle.'

I think of Lloyd's little caravan where he lives with a home-made wooden shack veranda by the river. You could fit it in the drawbridge of a castle.

'He won't like Norway then,' Dad says.

'No,' Lloyd says. 'I think he'll just go away.'

And I think, *We have flown thousands of miles away from everything and everyone we know and we are being attacked by Lloyd's crazy brother with weapons and a rifle grudge.*

Plan 2
The Newspaper

Going In

'Dad.'

'Yeah.'

I take my newspaper out. 'Let's go to the *Aftenposten*.'

He nods.

Lloyd salutes and zips his case back up.

I google the map and we go into town through exhaust fumes, tower blocks and shopping malls. I don't think there's even a dandelion growing here. OK, so Oslo isn't beautiful. But no one died of looking at uglyness.

Or plastic crossbows.

I put my headphones on and listen to:

apple-eating excitement

and stick my head down and walk.

We go through people stew and zoom and trams into the hard blue lights of the *Aftenposten*.

We crick our necks up at the glass-fronted tower block.

Lloyd shouts, 'DUCK,' and we drop down but nothing happens.

'False alarm,' he says. 'Sorry.' People stare at us. We get up off the pavement, dust the grit off our knees and push open the slick glass doors into a cool, skiddy hallway.

I look at Dad clutching his trumpet case. I look at Lloyd looking out the window for weapons.

I walk up to the desk.

A woman in a bun and blue suit is working on a computer.

Her fingers snacker on the keyboard.

'Can I speak to the editor, please?'

She looks down at me. 'Do you have an appointment?'

'No.'

'Then I do not think it is possible.' She squints and looks at Lloyd who is trying to rescue a bee out of the window with a bus ticket. 'He is very busy.'

'It's very important.'

'Mr Eriksen does many important things.' She starts to turn away.

'This is REALLY important.' I yell. 'Please.' I say.

I put my phone down on the desk.

And hit PLAY.

The music comes on.

And my video voice-over.

One boy. (A shot of my face.)

One newspaper. (A shot of the paper.)

And one regular random zoo bench. (Montage of a baby, a rhino, a shot of the black twiddly zoo gates.)

One mystery to solve.

One place to start.

With you,

The Aftenposten.

The guardian of the secret.

Only you can help this boy discover who he really is and why . . . (I point at my head.)

Will you help?

Will you not help and watch him go home . . . ?

All the way back to England.

With nothing.

And no money.

And crying . . .

She pushes the pause button. 'Are you serious?'

'I was found under this paper.' I put the paper on the desk. 'I have no idea who I am.' I point at a stain on the N. 'That bit's where I sicked up some milk.' I push the paper over. 'Imagine if it was you.' I look right at her.

She looks down at the date on it.

'It's all I've got. Seriously.' It is.

She looks up at me.

And picks up her phone.

She speaks in Norwegian. It sounds very up and downy. Like a word roller coaster.

Lloyd rescues the bee through the double doors and stands behind us. 'La de dah de dah de,' he whispers. Dad elbows him. I put my fingers in my mouth so I don't laugh.

She puts the phone down. 'Mr Eriksen will be here in one minute.'

I breathe out and a hot piece of satisfaction glows up from my stomach.

'Thank you.'

Dad smiles and we do a secret high five under the desk.

Lloyd wanders off to look at a picture of a farmer with a prize pig.

We watch the clock tick over.

CLUNK

    TICK

CLUNK

    TICK.

Dad whistles.

A man in a white shirt and black trousers arrives. He is smiley and nice. 'So you have come from England?' He opens his hands. 'Come in,' he says. 'Come in.'

We can't go in as the desk is in the way. We walk down both sides of it like we're on travelators set at the same speed and meet up at the end. 'You may leave you cases here,' he says and waves his hand. 'It is quite safe.' I think about Floyd. I check the CCTV – the cameras click round and look at us. I think about saying no.

But I don't.

Brain flick.

I want to know what he's going to tell us.

It's like Christmas when you go downstairs and open the presents.

You don't wait.

You get stuck in. Whether it's socks or not. You need to know ...

I watch my fingers leave my case.

Dad checks his watch.

Lloyd looks at Dad. 'How long will this take? Do we have time?'

'Sorry, do you not have time?' Mr Eriksen waves his hands.

'We have time,' Dad says and grabs Lloyd's arm and we follow the man down a corridor.

Tomatoes

The corridor is cool but not calm. People hurry past with papers and cups of coffee and phones.

We go into a side room and sit around a white table on leather chairs.

'So,' he says, 'how may I help you?'

I put the newspaper on the table. 'I was left under this as a baby.'

He whistles. 'Really, so.'

'I thought you might hold the secret of why.'

'Yes?'

'I thought the person who left it left it as a clue. So I could find them. So I could find out. Did you work here then?'

He nods.

Great.

'I wrote this one.' He points to the paper and translates: '"The new Svinesund bridge is opened joining Norway and Sweden". This was a nice moment.' He sighs and points to another page: '"Ten

are dead after an outbreak of legionnaires' disease".
This was a sad one.'

'Was anybody in the office pregnant? Did anyone leave unexpectedly?'

He shakes his head. 'Unfortunately not. Sorry. We have a distribution of over two hundred thousand. It could have come from anywhere, this paper.' He spreads his hands like they're the world.

'There must be something. There can't be nothing!' I look at Dad. There's no way this is it. I'm not going home now.

'I can help you!' Mr Eriksen taps his nose and takes a little white card and a gold pen out of his pocket. 'The birth registry,' he says, and writes it down. 'This is where you need to go.' He passes the card over. 'The information should all be in there.'

I take it. He slips his pen back in his pocket.

It won't be there. I looked it up online, like a million times. I haven't got a birth certificate. And no one knows what my other name was. No one knows who I was before I was Elvis. There's no way I can ask the birth registry. It's impossible.

Isn't it?

Maybe not.

The paper goes to two hundred thousand people right?

That isn't bad.

It's good.

Before the internet, people had papers.

Papers were the only way to spread news around.

'We could put an ad in,' I say.

Dad goes white. 'What?'

'An article – you could run a story. Boy found under paper seeks answers. After all these years. They'd see it then. They'd pick it up . . .'

Mr Eriksen strokes his chin. 'Yes,' he nods. 'Yes. Interesting.'

'No need,' Dad stands up. 'We have to go.'

'No way!' I stay sitting. 'Why?'

'It's private . . . It's . . .' He runs his hand through his hair.

Mr Eriksen shakes his head. 'I'm sorry,' he says. 'I'm sorry. I see you have a fine family.' He looks at Dad and Lloyd who is saving a spider from the plug socket. 'Sometimes we need to know our own secrets,' he says. 'But you know, we share sixty per cent of our DNA with tomatoes and we are nothing like tomatoes. You want a free paper?'

'Oh yes!' Lloyd puts the spider in a plant pot and takes three.

'No thanks.' I pick my birth one up off the table and stare at Dad. If he didn't want to come he should've said it. If he doesn't want me to know, why bother? I narrow my eyes and mouth, *what?*

He scratches his ear and mouths, *later.*

I get up and fold my arms.

Mr Eriksen walks us back down the corridor to our cases, past more people with coffee and phones and a woman who puts her hands through her hair and says, 'Aaaghhh,' and keeps walking.

None of us says anything.

We stop at the foyer. I look at my bag. It's moved. I know 'cos the handle's on the other side. Why?

Dad checks his watch. AGAIN.

'You are all OK?' Mr Eriksen says. His forehead wrinkles.

And Dad says, 'Yes thank you, thank you very much,' and grabs the bags and hustle-walks me out the door.

Hard Things and Secrets

We stand on the street and I hold the card.

Lloyd waves at pigeons.

Cars fly by. And people. And babies and dogs.

'What was that about?' I yell.

'Reasons,' Dad says and runs his hand through his hair.

I look up at the mountain of glass windows and think of how big the world is.

And how hard it is to try and find two people in it.

A man and a woman.

THEM.

People that could be anywhere.

People that could be anyone.

People that could be nowhere at all.

'Let's get an ice cream,' Dad says.

'No thanks.' I drop the card down the drain.

'It was a good plan,' he says.

'It was till you ruined it.'

'We are united! We are united!' Lloyd runs over and pats both our shoulders.

'There's something you should know.' Dad looks at his watch. AGAIN. 'We need to go.'

'Why?' I kick a rock off the pavement.

He hangs his head. 'There's something I should've told you a long time ago.'

Plan 3

Dad
the *actual* surprise

Reasons

'Like what?'

'Come on,' he says and walks off fast down the street.

Lloyd weaves in and out like a speedy weasel.

'Where are we going?' I run along behind.

'The bus station,' Dad yells over his shoulder. 'We're going back to the airport.'

I stop running. 'We're going home?' Someone bangs into the back of me. 'I'm not going home.'

'No.' Dad turns round. People bang into his sides and his bag. 'We're not.'

Lloyd jogs on the spot.

'We're going north,' Dad says. 'On a plane.'

I keep staring.

'A propeller one. Like Tintin. It leaves in two hours, OK?'

'Why?' People swarm around me. Secrets aren't Dad's thing. This is weird.

'Let's just get an ice cream, OK?' He rubs his head. 'We're all tired.'

'I'm not.'

'Do you want to miss the plane?'

'No.'

'I'll tell you then,' he says. 'I promise. Let's just get there, OK.'

I look at him. I think about a propeller plane. This is

A – a bit freaky

B – cool

C – weird, why?

I need to go. I want to go. Don't I?

'Do you trust me?' He holds a hand out.

I nod. I do. Always.

'OK,' I say.

'Onwards!' Lloyd says and runs off, fast, and trips over a curb and cuts his chin. I look around for green tweed. There is none. We stop the blood with a tissue and run back into the station. We check the bus-times board and get *softis* (Mr Whippy) from an orange shop with *Donald Duck* magazines and packets of Don't Stop and Can't Stop that look like M&Ms.

I know something is up as Dad lets me get as many toppings as I want. I get Smarties and marshmallows and chocolate raisins and jelly babies, but just the green ones and chocolate sauce and we sit down on red plastic chairs next to a big window.

'So?' My spoon hovers.

'So,' Dad says. 'I'm sorry we're doing this here. I wanted . . .' A man with plastic bags walks past us and shouts, 'The problem is the infrastructure!' and wanders off. 'I wanted it to be nice.' He sighs. 'Is your ice cream nice?'

I eat a spoon with Smarties. 'Yes,' I say, 'it is. Everything's nice.'

We ignore a couple having an argument by the ticket kiosk. The man kicks a suitcase and walks off. Lloyd tucks a napkin under his chin.

'Firstly,' Dad says, 'I wanted to tell you this before. I'm sorry I didn't. It was wrong.' He breathes out and puts an arm round me.

'When I found you on the bench it wasn't just the newspaper you had.'

'And the HELP vest.' I eat a green Smartie.

'It was also this.' He takes out a piece of paper from his pocket.

'What is it?' I look at Dad. I look at the paper.

'Plan B,' he says.

'You mean Plan C.'

'Yeah,' he sighs. 'Plan C. It's your birth address.'

Sorry

Dad's eyes go all red.

'I know it's weird,' he says. 'It's probably a shock.'

'Yeah.' I put down my spoon. 'It is.'

I stare at the paper.

'You've had that for twelve years?' I thought we were a team.

He rubs his forehead. 'Yes,' he says.

'And you never said.'

Lloyd spits out his lemony mineral water.

Dad puts his hands over his eyes.

None of us says anything for a minute.

Dad leaves the space for me to fill.

He could explain but he won't. He'll wait for me to ask.

To know what I want to know.

He'll wait till I'm ready.

'Why did you never tell me before?'

'I wanted to. But it was never the time,' he says. 'I thought when it was time you'd ask. And you did.' He rubs his eyes. 'I thought it'd be something we'd find out about when you wanted to. Now you want to.'

'I've always wanted to.'

'You never said.' Dad tilts his head.

'You let me go to the *Aftenposten*.' I feel like some eight-year-old that you let make dinner and then have a ready meal in the freezer just in case, 'cos you know you're never *really* gonna eat what they make.

'I didn't know . . .' Dad looks at Lloyd.

Lloyd looks down and mops the table.

'What?'

'I didn't know what it meant. Not for sure.' He rubs his eyes with the backs of his hands. 'I'm so sorry.'

I look at the ice cream. The colour's come off all the Smarties.

Sorry.

It's such a stupid word.

Sorry I forgot to switch off the TV.

Sorry I didn't take out the rubbish.

Sorry I forgot my homework.

Works.

But for this. For stuff like this there needs to be something so much **BIGGER**.

A Key

I tuck my hands in my armpits. I can feel the sweat.

Dad rubs his chin. 'I think . . .'

'What?'

'I think I didn't wanna be replaced.' His face crashes. He looks at the table. 'Which is stupid. I know.' He waves his hand and looks at me. 'You know in China there's a legend that when you're born you have invisible red strings attached to all the people who are going to be important to you in your life,' he says. 'They're all there before you even begin.'

I think about the invisible threads. I think about the dot-to-dot shapes in the stars. I think about clicking and clicking and clicking through YouTube. The link to a link to a link to a link. Click, click, click connections.

How you get from *Top 10 Scary Kids Who Remember Their Past Lives* to *Bad Lip-Reading Star Wars*.

'What does it say?'

'It says Skriva, 8320 Norway. It's an address. Their address. I think.' He breathes out. 'It's in the north.'

I think about the propeller plane. 'Does it say their names?'

'No.'

'Nothing about them?'

'No.'

'Who else knows?'

Dad looks at Lloyd. 'Just me,' Lloyd says.

'Honest?'

They nod.

'Good. I'd feel really stupid if I was the last person to know things about my own life.'

Dad pushes the paper over. 'Take it,' he says, 'it's yours.'

OK, so the *Aftenposten* wasn't the key.

This paper is.

How do you open a door with a paper key?

You stick it in your pocket.

And go.

'OK,' I say, 'let's get the bus before we miss the plane.' I put the ice cream on the table to curdle on its own. 'But no more secrets. I hate secrets.'

Dad nods. 'I'm sorry,' he says. 'It was wrong.'

'It was.'

We get up.

The numbers click round on the departure board.

The minutes click past to our plane.

Life can change in a click.

We have the address.

We have tickets.

We have a concrete plan in the concrete city.

It's possible.

It's actually suddenly possible.

And my heart starts to lift and hope floods back into me like hot water up a tea towel.

Stuck

Lloyd sits next to me on the bus and points to my pocket. 'Don't let anyone take that away – swear on your life!' He crosses his chest.

'It isn't a lottery ticket.' I smile. Actually in a way I guess it is. It's kind of like a life lottery ticket. I take a photo of it, just in case. Lloyd takes one too and tells me a story about the great Blondin who crossed Niagara Falls on a tightrope flipping pancakes and who said that the secret to tightrope walking is the first three steps.

'The first step is confidence,' Lloyd says. I think about getting on the plane to get here.

'The second is faith.' I think about the *Aftenposten*.

'The third leads you to your destiny.'

I think about the propeller plane and grip the compass.

The bus brakes hiss and we run into the airport terminal.

'How long have we got?'

'Twenty minutes.' Dad gets out the tickets in a little envelope.

I hold mine. It's long and thin with a checked pattern underneath and

```
Elvis Crampton Lucas
```

on top. I like seeing my name printed out. It feels weird but nice. Like looking at myself from the outside.

```
flight no: WD451
dept: 16.45
```

We walk up to the check-in desk.

The person behind it stands in a green uniform with a checked neck scarf and smiles.

'*Hei hei*,' she says. 'Tickets and passports please.'

I pass her my ticket.

Dad unzips the front of his case to get the passports out. He puts his hand in. When it comes out there aren't any passports in it.

He rubs his head.

He checks his pocket.

His other pocket.

His jacket.

He undoes his case and starts to look through everything. Jumpers and socks fall out.

'Dad.' People are staring.

'It won't be in there,' I say. 'We haven't even opened that yet.'

'We just had them,' Dad says. I scoop his jumpers and socks back in the case. And stare back at the staring people.

'I'm sorry, sir.' The person behind the check-in desk looks worried. We are frantic. 'I can't board you without passports.'

Dad puts both hands on his head. 'What time do you shut?'

'Fifteen minutes.'

'S***.'

'Dad!'

'What!'

A man pushes his case forwards into the back of my leg.

'Ow.'

Lloyd pushes it back. 'It isn't polite to push.'

'I'm afraid I'll have to ask you to stand aside.'

80

The check-in assistant looks behind us at the queue of people. She means all of us. 'You can try lost property.'

'Right.' Dad zips up his suitcase.

'To lost property!' Lloyd raises his arms and runs.

I clutch my ticket.

'What's gonna happen if we can't go?' I whisper.

'I don't know.'

We get to lost property and wait behind someone who's really angry about an umbrella.

They leave.

The man checks. Our passports aren't there.

'Isn't there someone you can ring?' Dad's head sweats.

He rings the security manager and shakes his head. 'Perhaps later, sir,' he says.

Dad bangs the desk. 'We haven't got time for later.'

The tannoy says, 'Would all passengers for flight WD451 please proceed to gate seventeen as this flight is now ready for boarding.'

I look at the ticket. That flight is us. I think hard. 'We must have left them somewhere else.'

'Where?'

I stare at the shiny black floor tiles. The world goes misty. I plug into my brain. And look back over everything. Following us through everywhere we've been.

The hot-dog stand.

The bus.

The street.

The newspaper office.

The newspaper office?

It's the only place we left the bags.

I look at Dad. 'We didn't lose them.'

'We did, Elvis.'

'We didn't.' I think about the turned-round cases. 'Someone took them.'

'Who?'

'The green man. The tweed man.' I look at Lloyd. 'Your brother.'

'Floyd?' Lloyd looks at the floor. 'No, I don't think so.'

'When?' Dad pulls his hair.

'When we were at the newspaper office. It's the only time we left the bags.'

'I'll buy us new ones,' Lloyd says.

'You can't buy us new ones,' Dad says.

'Did you get travel insurance?' Lloyd points a finger in the air. 'They replace passports with travel insurance.'

'How would you know?'

'Please stand aside, sir,' the lost-property man says. A man with a budgie in a cage stares at us. We move aside and sit down on metal seats with armrests that don't move. The bars dig into my legs.

'We could go to the police?' I say. 'Passports are serious. People care about people losing their identity.' I swallow. 'Identities are important.'

'Yes, it might have been people traffickers that took them,' Lloyd says.

'It wasn't people traffickers.' Dad slumps.

BING BONG. 'This is an announcement for all passengers on flight WD451. Please make your way to gate seventeen as this flight is about to depart.'

I think about our three empty seats. My heart is on that plane. My body is here.

Lloyd hangs his head. 'I'm sorry you have to go through this. My family is a disappointment.'

I wonder if we're being watched.

Is Floyd here?

Laughing at us?

'It took three weeks' wages to buy those tickets.' Dad puts his head in his hands. 'It's hopeless,' he says. 'Without passports, we can't even go home. We're completely stuck.'

Think

My brain starts fizzing like Mentos in Coke.

Frothy, frothy.

There must be a way out. There's always a way out.

I look at my watch.

I look at the ticket.

The clock ticks round.

I think fast but I'm too slow.

4.46

It's too late.

The plane's gone.

I imagine it taking off.

Sometimes when I have to make choices or things go wrong it's like there's another me that did the other thing. The one that practised the spellings and got ten out of ten. The one that said the right thing. The one that caught the plane. The other me flies off and looks out the window at the city zooming away. The other me feels sorry for the real actual-life me sitting on the hard metal seats.

I switch my brain on. There must be a way out. There's always a way out.

My fingers tap the armrest.

My feet tap the floor.

My brain cells tap into my brain.

Think.

I listen to the sound of:

silence thoughtful.

If Floyd took the passports, he's got them. Unless he's sold them? Or binned them?

Why would he steal them? If we find him we might get them back?

This is unlikely as it means:

A – Finding him. There're millions of people here and all we know is that he's wearing a green tweed jacket and have no proof he took them.

B – Even if we found him he could just deny it.

I keep tapping.

The passports aren't the problem.

The problem is the plane.

There're other ways to travel. We could've come here on a boat.

If you go on a train or a boat you don't need a passport.

Not inland anyway.

Passports are for borders.

If you stay in the border you can go where you want.

'We can catch a train or a bus or a boat instead,' I say. 'Other things go north. If we go on those we don't need a passport.'

Dad looks at his watch. 'Now?'

'We can find somewhere to stay and get the tickets tonight. It'll be better than flying.' He looks hurt. 'Not that flying's not good, it's just we'll see things. We'll get to see everything on the ground, not like someone's just dropped us out of the sky.' This is the first holiday of my life. I actually want to see it. 'You've got money haven't you, Lloyd?'

'Yes,' Lloyd says and gets a load out.

Dad puts his hand over to cover it up. 'Put it away.'

'Right.' I get my phone out. 'Let's book an Airbnb. We're staying in Oslo.'

Hedgehog Lover

We make Lloyd a profile on Airbnb with a photo of him in front of a bendy metal sculpture on the airport Wi-Fi.

Lloyd Partington
I am an independent man with independent thoughts.
I like people, nature and apples.
Show me your world. I am always interested.

Then we have to make one for Dad because Lloyd doesn't believe in credit cards and Airbnb doesn't do cash.

He pulls me into his selfie. 'You make me look more human,' he says. He looks smiley and nice. 'People get put off by the moustache.'

'Like who?'

He shrugs.

We write his profile.

George Lucas (not that George Lucas)
Dad of Elvis (not that Elvis)

I look at him. 'You really want to put that?'

'Yeah. I wouldn't be me without you!'

'Really?'

'True blue.'

This makes me tear up a bit so I look back at the screen. 'Right.'

He types . . .

Lover of music and hedgehogs.

'You don't want people to think you're a hedgehog-lover.'

He shrugs. 'It'll do.'

'It sounds *wrong*. There's other things you like.'

'There isn't time.'

I hope no one I know sees it. Ever.

We look for places to stay and I find a cheap one (on Dad's card) with a room with a photo of a bike and a woman with a purple headscarf who says:

People think my city is ugly. I will show you it isn't!
Mulki Hosseini

'She looks nice.'

Dad looks over my shoulder. 'Yeah,' he says and clicks on 'instant book' and gets a map.

Lloyd stands up. 'Back to the *Flybussen*!' he says.

And we groan and salute him as this is how things are done.

Shadows

The flat has a dark staircase that leads up to a red glass door. The bike from the picture is on the wall inside. I press the bell. A shadow behind the door spreads out to meet us. The chain unfastens, the lock unlocks.

For a minute I hold my breath. The door opens.

'*Hei hei!*' Mulki says. She is smiley and nice.

What did I expect?

Floyd's shadow hangs in my mind.

We go in and have to take our shoes off by the door. 'It's a Norway thing,' she says and pulls a face. 'We all do it.' Her socks are bright blue. The floorboards are all polished wood.

It is good for sock skidding.

I slide down the hall and into a bright, planty lounge and into the bedroom with all our stuff. She gives us a key and shows us an information folder. 'My home is your home!' she says and leaves.

We skid into the kitchen. There are racks and

racks of glass jars and spices. Dad cooks egg-fried rice for dinner. I sit on a footstool and look at the takeaway menus in the information folder and play guess the price. *Fritystekt kyllingilet med sursot saus* (deep-fried chicken with sweet-and-sour sauce) costs seventeen pounds each. We eat our rice.

Mulki comes in while we are washing up. 'How are you liking Oslo?' she says.

'We've only been on the *Flybussen* really,' I say.

'Three times.' Lloyd dries and stacks the plates.

I think about her ad: *People think my city is ugly. I will show you it isn't!*

'I don't mean to be rude, but I think it is ugly actually.' I shrug.

'OK,' she says. She doesn't look mad. 'You are not alone!' She looks at Dad in the Marigolds. 'You are finished?'

He snaps the gloves off and nods. Lloyd stacks the last plate.

'Good. I will show you just how beautiful Oslo can be.'

'I believe in giving everything a second chance.' Lloyd dries the wet patches on his shirt with a tea towel.

Dad rubs his eyes. 'OK,' he says. 'OK.'

'Great,' Mulki says.

I think of seeing something that isn't concrete.

I think if Floyd's got our passports what else does he want?

The best way to avoid him is movement.

That's what they do in films.

Right?

The Tiger City

We follow Mulki out into the streets full of people and sound. I tune my ears in. Feet, tyres, brakes, talking and rumble that rises up out of the belly of a city like a cloud.

We follow the streets and roads to wooden walkways and a river. 'This is the Akerselva,' she says and we walk down it past waterfalls and over bridges, and I think about the city breathing and the river keeping it alive and pumping out clean air. We buy a slice of spice cake each with icing as thick as our thumbs and eat them next to a church with bells that chime like music boxes and woodchoppers and palaces and death.

Birds hop in and out looking for crumbs and I feed some of my cake to a sparrow and Dad says, 'That cost five quid.'

And Lloyd says, 'Love is more than money.'

And the sparrow looks pleased and hops off.

'Oslo has two hundred and twelve sculptures and

many parks,' Mulki says. 'The beauty is there, you just have to look for it.'

'Like life,' Lloyd says.

'Exactly.'

We walk down to the fjord where the river opens out into bigger water and finds what it is looking for. I think of it sighing out when it gets there. I think about us running north.

Fairy lights click on in between the lamp posts.

And Mulki shows us a sculpture of a paving slab with an army of miniature people hiding underneath it.

I think about things underneath things.

Things that are hidden.

That you have to looks sideways to see.

Like when you lift a rock up and a millipede springs out.

You should expect it but you don't – it's always a surprise.

I don't see any weird shadows or green jackets.

And I wonder if Floyd got what he wanted with the passports.

And I link Dad's arm and record the sound of:

being happy to be lost in something new.

And I think happiness is like sparklers. Bright and fizzy and gone quicker than you expect and I keep a lookout for flamethrowers.

Complicated

Back in the flat Mulki helps us to book the train tickets.

'Do you work in travel?' Lloyd asks.

She laughs. 'No. I'm a human rights lawyer,' she says.

'The world needs all the help it can get.' Lloyd kneels on a chair and she nods.

'I do my best. I see so much more than I am able to take on. It's frustrating.' She moves her hands like she wants to join them. 'I do the Airbnb as it brings people together.'

'Like us.' I click on the train site.

'Yes,' she nods. 'Like you.' She feeds Colin, her guinea pig, and we buy tickets for trains that go all the way up to the north. One train, one sleeper. I look at photos of the compartments with little water bottles and square chocolates and bunks and their own sinks.

I look at the times. 'It takes eighteen hours. Seriously?'

Mulki laughs. 'Yes seriously,' she says.

I have a turn with Colin on my knee. He's hot and squeaks.

'Then we get a car,' Dad says. 'And a ferry.'

I look at the map. At the bobbing island in the middle of nowhere. My island.

I wish I could plug in my brain and see what I saw then.

I wish brains were like hard drives.

Mulki shows us photos of some sculptures we missed. Two kids riding their mum like a horse and a man kicking kids off his legs.

'You think my city is ugly now?' she says.

'It's interesting ugly,' I say and we put Colin back in his house.

She smiles and goes out for a run and I have a bath and thoughts swirl around in my brain.

I think about Floyd and Lloyd and make a tower of bubbles. I think that everything basically comes down to three things:

A – What did Floyd want the passports for?

and

B – Why is he trying to scare Lloyd?

and

C – How exactly does he know where we are?

I split the bubble pile in two and think about me and my parents.

The piles drift apart.

And float back together again.

Like us.

Getting closer.

I get out and my thoughts go down the plughole. I can feel the heat coming up through my feet on the green glass tiles.

In the bedroom Dad opens the window and squats next to the camp bed. I get in. It traps my arms by my sides like I'm in a drainpipe.

'You OK?' he says.

'I feel like a ruler.'

'You want my bed?'

'Nah. It's OK.' I want him to be happy and comfy. 'Mulki's nice.' I try to wriggle my arms. 'Do you wish you had someone?'

'I've got you,' he says.

'I don't mean me,' I say.

'It's difficult isn't it.'

'Is it?'

'Yeah,' he says, 'it is. Now go to sleep.'

He hums 'La Bamba' and goes into the lounge with the bottle of whisky and a book.

I lie there and listen to the sound of the city outside, and the clock and the pigeons and cars and people going off places with clacking shoes and laughing, till a stone flies in through the window gap and lands on the floor.

There is a note tied around it. The note says:

I am going to kill you.

I take it through to the lounge. Dad looks up from his book.

Lloyd stops stroking the plants.

And I say, 'Lloyd, why did you fall out with Floyd?'

And Lloyd says, 'It's complicated.'

About Lloyd Partington

As long as I've known, there's always been a Lloyd Partington. Jumping in and out of our house and our windows. Planting a new apple tree every July and telling Mr Singh what a great job he's doing with his bees. (I asked him if bees are really that important and he said yes, bees fertilise apple trees and without them we'd be *destroyed*.) Living in a caravan with a wood burner and a home-made veranda extension on the front, by the river in a field. Sometimes with rat infestations. Sometimes without.

I didn't know how much I didn't know about him until now.

I didn't know he even had a brother.

Or a castle.

Sometimes the things you don't know open up in front of you like strange presents that you don't really want but have to pretend to like, and people you know feel like places you don't know.

In my head I imagine a 3D hologram of Lloyd spinning in a spy-film green light with stats typed out in computer writing underneath.

Lloyd: friend
History: unknown

Roll Over

'Lloyd,' I say. 'How dangerous is Floyd? Seriously.'

'He's three times national champion at rifle shooting,' Lloyd says. 'But now he hasn't got a rifle.'

'He's got a crossbow.'

'I don't know where he got the crossbow.'

'And our passports.' I hold up the note. 'And rocks.'

'Can't you just say sorry?' Dad says.

'About what?'

'About selling the Winchester.'

'We haven't spoken since my dad died.' He looks at the floor. 'Ten years ago.'

'I don't like getting attacked,' Dad says.

'We just need to be observant.' Lloyd lifts a ladybird out of a plant pot. 'He won't follow us everywhere. Floyd gets bored. Eventually. Eventually he'll just go back home.'

Dad's face looks pointy. He shuts the window and we all go to bed.

I put my headphones on and listen to:

being happy to be lost in something new.

And try to get back to my happy place.
But my head keeps saying:
I'm going to kill you.
I put my headphones round my neck.
'Does he mean it, Lloyd?' I whisper.

'I don't know,' he whispers back. 'When I was nine I accidentally trod on his Hornby train set and he took my pocket money for two years afterwards for repayments.' Lloyd closes his eyes and rolls over. 'Scaring people's all Floyd knows.'

And I think Floyd is going to be around for as long as it takes.

And I roll
    around
        and around
     and around.

And I must get to sleep at some point 'cos I wake up.

Brain Scuttle

I look at the clock. 2.23.

Something's in my mind and won't let go.

I pick my jeans up off the floor and creep into the lounge.

The moon is up and the street is full of gentle rumble.

If anyone is out there, they're shuffling.

I take my birth address and the stone note from my pocket.

Colin scrabbles about in his house.

The birth address is crisp and folded and keeps trying to close back up like a hand.

The rock note's crumpled and a mess, like it's trying to hide its words in the cracks.

I put them on the glass table, smooth out the paper and look at the writing.

Blue biro.

Black felt marker.

They're both completely different.

Apart from the Ks.

Bending down with flicky-up ends.

The Ks are exactly the same.

EXACTLY.

EXACTLY.

EXACTLY.

I look at

    I'm going to *k*ill you.

and

    S*k*riva.

Maybe it doesn't mean anything.

Maybe lots of people write weird Ks?

But I hate the feeling that Floyd and my birth address are in *any way* connected.

Creepy Feeling

Mulki has already gone to work when we get up. She's left a note with her mobile number and cheese and crackers and juice and raisin buns with dark red raspberry jam. We eat and crunch with cups of tea.

Dad wraps some buns up in cling film for later, then we pack up. I write, *Thanks!* on the blackboard wall in the kitchen. Lloyd picks up the chalk and writes:

Tusen Tak, Lloyd

I stare at it. The K is the same as Floyd's.
EXACTLY.
EXACTLY.
EXACTLY.
Lloyd looks at me looking. 'It means thanks very much,' he says.

'OK,' I say. Right, so do loads of people have weird flicky Ks?

We put the key under the mat and walk back out into the world.

The people sea is sweeping down the street. We step into it. The sun is bright and twinkly. We give coins to people who look hungry and have signs we can't read and avoid a suspicious flying golf ball from behind a billboard.

Lloyd squat-runs with his hands over his head. 'Run, Elvis, run!' he says.

Dad turns round and shouts into the air, 'I'm not running!'

I pull him along.

'I hate bullies,' Dad says.

I try to shrug off the creepy feeling of being watched.

'Maybe we should just pretend we're on a different platform?' I whisper to Lloyd. 'Then sneak off on to another one.'

'Yes.' He nods.

'No!' Dad says and helps a kid who's just fallen over by the vending machine. 'No running, no hiding. If Floyd's got something to say, he can say it to our face.'

'What if he punches our face?'

'He won't,' Dad says. 'He's a bully. Bullies don't take on gangs.' He puts his hand on Lloyd's shoulder. 'We're your gang, Lloyd.'

'Hmmn.' Lloyd squeezes his eyes shut and just misses a lamp post, and we speed-walk past two men balancing on invisible sticks and homeless people with magazines which Dad buys, even though we can't understand them, into the archy mouth of the station and into three seats heading north.

Dots to the Left Mean You're a Procrastinator

On the train the seats go in single rows of two on each side. I sit on my own behind Lloyd and Dad.

I snap the footrest down and we clunk off.

I use the train Wi-Fi to google:

What does your handwriting actually say about you?

And find out that:

Narrow L loops mean you may be restricting yourself, which could lead to feelings of tension

and:

Rounded letters mean you are creative and artistic.

But nothing about weird flicky Ks.

I hope my letters are rounded.

I watch out the window and try to make videos of mountains that go up and up and water that throws itself off the top and lakes and jetties and forests but the tunnels keep getting in the way.

Tree blur

    Black

        Lake

            Black

                Bush

I think about Floyd.

If he wanted to kill Lloyd, he'd have done it by now. But he didn't.

I think about animals.

Animals threaten each other when they want to mate or when they're scared, if they've got something to hide. Like a den with cubs or its babies. I learnt that at the zoo. People are basically animals. Rats wash more than humans.

Humans threaten you when they're scared. Of what?

What does Floyd care about?

People?

Him and Lloyd haven't spoken in years. If he was bothered, he would have sorted it. He didn't.

Money? He lived in a castle.

He must have had money.

Lloyd doesn't.

I tap Lloyd's head. 'Lloyd, how come you don't have any money if you lived in a castle?'

'I invested it, in other things.'

'Like what?'

'Good causes.'

That figures.

And I think:

1 – Floyd stole the passports not the money.

2 – Floyd said he was going to kill Lloyd, but he didn't. He didn't try to kill us – he tried to scare us.

3 – People can't travel without passports. If people are scared they go home.

Floyd wants us to go home?

WHY?

The train stops at a yellow wooden station and a boy with a massive rucksack and cool Afro hair gets on and sits next to me.

'I'm Bjorn,' he says.

'I'm Elvis,' I say. 'Not *that* Elvis.'

'Not what Elvis?'

'It doesn't matter.'

'You are from England?'

'Yeah.'

'Cool.'

He shares his paprika crisps and tub of spicy nuts and shows me a game he's made on his phone called

Chainsaw Badger – it's actually great. You have to run out of the way of the chainsaw.

'I want to be a programmer,' he says.

I shrug. 'Nice.' I show him one of my videos. He laughs at the bit with the snail eyes.

'Sick. You've been on a train in Norway before?'

'No.'

'OK,' he says. 'Let's go,' and we walk down the carriages in our socks and press buttons to go in and out of doorways and into the buffet car with red plastic seats and posters of waffles and people serving behind a shiny silver bar. We look at Coke and meatballs and things in the click-down fridge cabinets that we have no money for. We lean in close to see what our reflections look like in the silver worktop. Our noses look massive. Bjorn makes some horns with a serviette and I make giraffe ears.

'Can I help you?' the person behind the counter says. We shake our heads and back away.

'Let's do Train Run,' Bjorn says.

'What's that?

'This.'

We bomb it through the train playing Train Run, where you run as fast as you can along the carriage

113

and try not to fall over on to people. The train grinds on the rails underneath us. My feet wobble. I try to keep up. I slip and grab a seat. I miss a baby's head. We go round a bend. I balance to the right. We go into a tunnel and my head spins in the dark and we fall over in the bendy, joiny section and Bjorn shouts,

'*BRAK*.'

'What?'

'It means crash.'

'*BRAK*,' we shout. No one even looks at us.

'Trains are so long in Norway no one cares,' Bjorn says.

We play Train Run until our third *BRAK* and Bjorn tears a hole in his knee and bleeds through his jeans. I bang my head on a railing.

I think about Lloyd banging and bleeding.

'Someone wants to kill my dad's best friend,' I say.

'Who?' He pokes the blood. I watch the red spread out over his dark skin.

'His brother.'

'I wish I could kill my brother.'

'Really?'

'Yes and no,' he says. 'He's so annoying.'

'How old is he?'

'Eight.'

'Hmmn.'

'He might not mean it.' He rubs at the blood.

'He shot at us with a crossbow.'

'OK.' He shrugs. 'People do a lot of hunting in Norway.' He licks the blood off his finger. 'But not usually people.'

'No.'

'How does he follow you?'

'He watches,' I say, 'I think. Actually, I don't know.' I look round like I might get sprung and tell Bjorn everything

The bench.

The paper.

The passports.

My birth address.

He listens and looks out the window. 'If I were you I'd ring it.'

'What?'

'The address. It feels connected.' He spits on his finger. 'Floyd and you.'

'It isn't connected.' I push the thought away like a nettle. I don't mention the Ks.

He gets out his phone. Chainsaw Badger bounces along the screen. The trees run out of the way of the chainsaw. 'When I made this, I made the badger follow the trees by programming them to go to the same place. You think he's coming to get you . . . so you run away. Actually you're just going in the same direction. Get it?'

'No.'

'Maybe he isn't following you. Maybe you're both going to the same place. Stop going and see if he follows you.' He puts it back in his pocket.

'How does he know where we're going? Him and Lloyd fell out. They don't speak.'

Bjorn shrugs. 'Maybe he needs to follow you to get there.' He gets up.

I press the door button. It hisses. 'Maybe Lloyd's lying. Maybe they do speak.'

'Why would he lie?'

'I dunno.'

And we walk back down the train and I think it's funny how you can meet someone for three hours and talk about everything.

And know someone for years and not.

116

Off

We get back to our seat and Bjorn starts putting all his stuff in his rucksack. The train pulls up to the station. 'This is my stop.' He writes his number on the back of my hand. I write mine on the back of his and we bump knuckles goodbye.

A woman with grey hair and snow boots climbs off a four-by-four quad bike and trailer to meet him. I watch him on the platform and wave.

He waves back and goes. The train pulls away.

I wonder if he is one of my life threads, if we were meant to meet?

I think about what he said. And watch *Ten Ways To Know If Someone Is Lying*.

The altitude gets higher. The temperature gets lower. It doesn't feel any colder. The sunshine through the window is burning my arms. I wonder how that's possible. We stop and a man gets on with skis and poles and an army backpack. There are icicles in his moustache. The train climbs up and up into the mountains.

And suddenly I just want to get off. I want to be out there. In the waterfalls and bike tracks bouncing into forests and bright red cabins. Not trapped in here.

I tap Dad on the shoulder. He turns round.

'I wanna get off.'

Lloyd looks chuffed to bits. 'Let's get off!' He jumps up.

Dad looks worried. 'You wanna get off?'

'Yeah.'

'Why?'

'I just do.' I look at the snow. 'I want to be out there,' I say. 'Plus, we can ditch Floyd.'

'I'm not running away from Floyd.' Dad slides his phone into its case.

'Is he on the train?' Lloyd looks around like a meerkat.

'I don't know.' I shake my head. I don't. I don't even know what he looks like.

'Don't you wanna be out there, Dad?' We look at the mountains and bubbling streams bouncing by, white froth spraying.

The announcement says the train will stop in three minutes. *Platform on the right.*

Lloyd starts pulling his bag down off the rack.

Dad doesn't. His forehead wrinkles. He looks at the man with the icicle moustache. 'We've got no snow clothes.'

'We have vests.'

'We have no idea where we are,' he says.

I read the display screen. 'We're in Tilse,' I say. 'We can get another train tomorrow.' My heart starts to panic. 'You said if I wanted to stop we'd stop. I wanna stop.'

He strokes the side of his trumpet case. 'You wanna run wild in the mountains?'

'Yes!' I nod. 'Yes!'

'OK,' he says and smiles. 'Let's do it.'

The train starts to slow. I look at the mess on my seat. I try to cram it all into my bag. Shove shove shove. I push my feet into my shoes, put my iPod in my pocket. I grab my coat.

It stops. Lloyd straddles the platform and the train with his legs and presses the door-open button over and over and over again. The doors jerk open, shut, open, shut, open, shut on his trousers.

Our cases are stuck behind a massive black one.

We try to struggle them out.

We push and pull.

The guard blows his whistle.

They pop out.

We fall on the floor.

Dad shouts, 'WAIT!' and gets up and Lloyd throws himself out the way and we jump off the train. The guard tuts and the final whistle goes and the train zooms off. I don't see Floyd anywhere.

Do I?

A man in a black leather hat walks off quickly.

There is no green tweed.

We stand there in the wind.

My breath blows out in cold smoke.

My teeth chatter.

The cold bites into my arms and legs.

Lloyd puts his extra tracksuit bottoms on over his tracksuit bottoms.

I put on two extra T-shirts and my fleece.

The station flags flap about and bang the pole. The wind drills into our ears.

People disappear like ants down a hole and suddenly we are alone in an empty, blowy wilderness.

Me and Lloyd look at Dad. Our visible skin has gone bright pink.

Dad looks around like an owl looking for answers. 'What's next, McDuff?'

'A hotel?' I say.

Lloyd taps his pouch and nods.

And Dad says, 'Yeah to a hotel,' and ruffles my hair, and we follow the sound of twanging flag poles into the only building around.

Can't Things Be Nice for Once?

The building isn't a hotel. It's a tourist information centre and it's shut.

We all look at each other and shiver.

Lloyd hails down a taxi by standing in the middle of the road and I say, 'To a hotel please.'

And the man says, 'Which one?'

And I say, 'A cheap one.'

And the driver whistles through his teeth and drives off

He takes us to one with a wooden front and a light-up sign that isn't lit up.

We go up the steps and into the reception. It smells of plug-in air freshener and lemon wet wipes. I stare at the paintings of bullfights and hunting and whale catching that are all over the walls.

The hotel man has black curly hair and a deep voice like a gangster. 'How long?' he says.

We stare at him.

'How many nights?'

'Just the one,' Dad says and pulls a dead face when the man bends over and I try not to laugh.

'Fill this out.' He gives Dad a form on a clipboard.

Name
Address
Telephone number
Passport number

I stare at that last one.

'I'll fill it out later,' Dad says.

'You fill it in tonight.'

'Yes,' Dad says. 'Tonight.'

The man stares at both of us.

'I will pay,' Lloyd says and gets out his wedge of cash.

The man looks at the cash and takes it plus extra for a key deposit.

'Bathroom's down the hall,' he says, and points and hands us keys with wooden ladles on the ends. We walk off to drag the bags up the stairs.

I nudge Dad. 'Why did you say that?'

'About what?'

'The form. You can't.'

He sighs and shrugs. 'I just want things to be nice, Elvis. Can't things just be nice. For once?'

'You should've told the truth.' I heave up the case. 'It'll be fine.'

We stop on the landing.

The black-leather-hat man slides into room number fifty-two. Lloyd waves. He doesn't wave back.

Dad unlocks our door.

The room has just enough space for two beds and a hotplate with a saucepan and kettle by the window. The wallpaper over the hotplate is peeling off. The lampshade is brown. The bedspreads are grey. The carpet has black bits in.

Lloyd unlocks his door and says, 'Well this is lovely.'

And Dad shoves the cases in and locks it again and says, 'Let's go out, eh.'

Who I'd Be Without You

We walk fast past the reception man and his pictures of death and dark green velvet curtains.

'Afternoon!' Lloyd says and waves.

I drag him outside. 'Ow!' Lloyd rubs his arm.

'I don't like that man.'

'Why?'

'I don't like the way he stares at us. I don't like the way he never smiles. I don't like the photos of bulls being stabbed and trapped animals he has on his walls.'

Lloyd taps his Against Animal Cruelty badge. 'I'm very proud,' he says.

We stand on the pavement and breathe in lungfuls of clean crispy non-air-freshener air. The sun heats my skin.

'Wildness here we come!' Dad says and we go under an underpass and follow a path over bouncy wooden rope bridges and white-water streams which I leap over two jumps at a time and Dad says, 'Chase yer.' Dad tags me and I scream and get Lloyd, and we run for fun and to keep warm until Dad gets a stitch. He bends over. Our breath steams out and gets mixed up with snow clouds round the mountains.

It feels like being in a car advert.

Beautiful.

And wild.

Two people with hats with flaps and a dog like a bear walk past and stare at us. Lloyd asks if we can pet the dog and they say, '*NEI.*'

'What's blue and white and cold all over?' Dad says.

'Us?'

'An ice lake.' He points up ahead.

We go up to the lake. It's ice at the edges. Slushy mush in the middle.

I put my hand on the ice and poke my finger in to make a hole. I feel the sting of the water on my fingers. I feel it till I can't feel it any more. I put my fingers in my mouth to warm them back up. They taste of metal and nosebleeds and they numb my tongue.

There's a hiss and a rumble. One bark, then two,

three, four, five. I turn round. A blur of fur and eyes is snowballing along the road towards us. Kicking up grit and gliding. Six dogs tethered to each other. Tongues lolling. Eyes bright. Muscles rippling. Grey and white fur stood out against the cold. Puffed and prickly. They zoom along. We are hypnotised.

A man on a box with giant wheels bobbles along behind, holding on like a water skier.

'*Hei hei*,' he says.

They swoosh past.

We watch them thunder away down the road. Silence.

Dad scratches his head. 'We all saw that, right?'

'The world is alive with natural wonders.' Lloyd stretches his arms like he's talking to God.

'This place is magic,' I say and scoop up a bit of snow and chuck it at Dad.

Then we all scrape up bits of snow and chuck them at each other.

Dad takes a photo of me next to a snow pole. I point at it going over my head. I imagine living in this place with roads like snow caves. It's weird what happens in the world that you don't see. And how what's normal just depends on where you're born.

This could've been me. Couldn't it? I wonder if my bench parents like the cold?

We follow tiny pattery footprints to a furry thing that looks like a frothy guinea pig.

'Lemming,' Dad whispers and stands in the middle of the road while it crosses so it doesn't get squashed.

The lemming trots off down a hole and we run down the street past a guy on rollerboot skis going up and down the pavement in a Lycra ski suit, and buy tins of soup with orange labels and sticky cinnamon buns from the only shop there is and swing back through the hotel doors.

The reception man is not at the desk. I breathe out. When I go round the corner I see him talking on the phone. He stares at me and looks away.

'Sleep tight.' Lloyd scratches his head and shakes his soup and goes into his room.

We go into ours and heat the soup up on the hotplate in the saucepan.

I don't know what it is, but it's the best soup ever.

I bite into a cinnamon bun. It is buttery sweet and delicious. The sugar sticks my fingers to the top.

We open the window to let the soup smell

mingle with the crispy mountain air. I think if the mountains sang they'd sound like a finger on the rim of a wine glass. Pure and zingy.

I think about Bjorn. *If I were you I'd ring it.*

I think about Dad. *Can't things just be nice. For once?*

I think about being free in a place like this where no one knows you and you can be anything you want.

I could look up the number.

But I don't want to.

I just want to be here.

One day won't make any difference.

Will it?

We put our hands on the radiator. I look at the holes in the carpet.

'I'm glad we stopped.' Dad puts his arm round me. 'You can't just take pictures,' he says. 'You need to be in them. You have to live a bit.' We stare out past the dancing curtains.

He stands up and shouts out the window, 'I FEEL ALIVE.' He raises an eyebrow at me. 'How about you?"

I stand up and stick my head out. 'I FEEL ALIVE TOO!' I shout.

And he picks up his trumpet and plays jazz into the wind and I drum on the radiator with a teaspoon and record:

Us
(a trumpeting, dinging, humming-snow
mountain, laughing kind of sound).

And I wonder if playing music is something that's in my blood?
Or if it's something I got off Dad?
And I wonder who I'd be without it.
And I wonder who I'd be without

him.

Happy?

I sit up. The sun's coming in through the curtains.

'Morning.' I pull them open and look at the fresh snow on the mountaintops.

Sugar dust on granite.

Dad grunts and rubs his eyes. 'Hot chocolate?' he says.

'We don't have any.'

'Wanna bet?' He leans over the edge of the bed and gets a plastic bag of sachets out of his suitcase.

I smile and we put the kettle on and empty the powder out of the mini plastic packet and into an elephant mug and put boiling water in. It tastes sweet and thin, not thick and dark like Aunty Ima's. But it is still good. I dunk the floaters with my spoon.

Dad opens the curtains and sings . . .

'It's a new dawn,
It's a new day,
It's a new life for me,
And I'm feeling good.'

And has a bit of a dance.

He looks happy.

'I can't remember the last time I had a holiday,' he says.

'We've never had one,' I say.

'We've been camping.'

'You set the tent on fire.' I avoid the last bit of the chocolate that's all dusty.

He cocks his head. 'It was just a little singed hole.'

'I like happy you,' I say and smile.

'Me too,' he says and flicks his jumper on my head. 'Let's go get some breakfast before he disappears and hungry me gets out.'

Troll

Dad takes a shower first.

I log into the hotel Wi-Fi and think about ratings. Maybe that is how we see everything, how people judge people. We rate each other with stars.

Five-star friend.

Four-star friend.

They just don't write them down. And no one ever says so.

You're just supposed to know it.

I think about Bjorn and give him five stars.

I give Chainsaw Badgers 4.5.

And look up the train time out of here.

10.35

It's 8.15.

I look up YouTube.

There's a whole new batch of red thumb downers.

I scroll down to the comments.

One thumb downer is talking to another one.

It's kinda weird people talking about me that don't even know me.

What the **** is this crap?

Tell it how it is!

He's the kind of kid who kills his own cat, right?

Cat or Mom?

LOL

I thought Elvis was dead?

Ha! Elvis – do us a favour. Go die so we don't have to put up with any more of your ****.

Worst **** I've seen all year

Thumbs up if you agree!

Dad comes in.

I don't say anything. I just show him the string. If they think it, who else thinks it? Is that what everybody thinks?

'Don't listen to them, Elvis. These guys are just sick-heads with nothing better to do.' He holds my chin up. 'They're just jealous. Don't let it get to you. OK?'

I nod.

But it does.

It gets right into me. Into a place I can't get to.

I chuck my phone on the bed.

And I think I never want to make another video again.

Ever.

Empty?

We knock on Lloyd's door. He is dressed and ready. 'No rocks,' he says and points to the window, which isn't broken. 'Or death threats.'

'Lovely,' Dad says and grabs my hand and we go down the stairs and into the dining room.

It's big and white with a green carpet and a long table with a cloth and plates with squares of cheese and ham and fruit and fresh bread rolls and jugs of coffee and juice.

The rest of the dining room is empty.

And still.

'Do you think it's poisoned?' I look at all the dead animal heads mounted on the wall.

Dad laughs and fills his plate.

I pick up a strange fish thing. 'What's this?'

'Herring,' Dad says.

I get other stuff.

We sit down and I put squares of cheese and ham into a crispy white roll and spread it thick with butter. 'Why is no one else here?' I look at my plate but don't eat anything.

Lloyd nibbles a herring off a fork. 'Perhaps they're early risers.'

I look at my watch. 'It's half past eight.'

KNOCK, KNOCK.

A man's voice says, 'Hello,' and I think great, actual guests.

I turn round and see the black uniform, the black hat, the handcuffs and truncheon on the belt. Policemen guests?

'Good morning.' They look at Dad. They walk over to our table. 'I'm afraid we're going to have to ask you to come with us,' they say.

Not guests.

Policemen.

Sorry

Dad's cup of coffee hovers halfway to his mouth. 'Why?' He takes a sip.

'Finish your breakfast,' they say. 'We are not uncivilised.'

Dad looks confused. Lloyd looks terrified. My head is buzzy with questions.

The policemen turn round and pour themselves cups of coffee from the jug and talk in Norwegian.

'It'll be fine,' Dad whispers.

We eat in silence. Kind of. Me and Lloyd don't eat anything. Dad eats his really slowly. I don't know how he's hungry. My stomach has shrunk to a blip.

I stare at him. 'I haven't done anything,' he says and eats more ham. 'They can wait, OK.'

I think about the form, I think about the passport. I think about the mean starey reception man with his death pictures and animal heads. 'You didn't do the form.'

'You don't get arrested for that.'

Don't you? 'You're not actually arrested.' I pick my fingers under the table. 'If you were arrested you'd be in handcuffs.'

We get up, the policemen don't handcuff him. This is good.

'I'm coming!' I say and stand up. I'm not being left here on my own.

'We need you too, sir.' They look at Lloyd.

'Of course,' Lloyd says and stands, and his fingers muddle together and drop his napkin.

We walk out into the hallway. The policeman tips his hat to the reception desk man and says something in Norwegian that I don't understand.

I stare at the reception man. Hard. I wish I had laser eyes and could burn his hair off. It was him. I know it was him. And even though my eyes can't set things on fire, I give him a look that says, you'll be sorry. You'll be really very sorry.

I just don't know how to make him, yet.

Tick Tick Tick

I look at my watch as we pull into the police station.

'Don't worry,' Lloyd says biting his nails and spitting them on the floor. 'Everything will be fine.'

We go in.

It's very clean and white. We write our names in a book on the desk.

'You have photo identification?' They look at Dad.

'What for?' Dad looks in his wallet.

'A driving licence, a passport.' Policeman one says.

Dad puts his driving licence down on the desk.

'I don't even have a wallet, I just have this!' Lloyd shows everyone his travel pouch.

'You have no way of proving your identity?' Policeman two, the tall one, looks at Lloyd.

'No.'

'This way please.' We follow them into a smaller white room with a table and four chairs, two on each side. I stand at the back. 'You can sit outside.' They point at me.

'No thanks.' I'm not going anywhere.

Policeman one says, 'You did not fill out the hotel's identification document?'

I look at Dad. I *know*.

'It isn't a crime,' he says.

'It's a legal requirement.'

'Not at Airbnbs,' I say.

'Airbnbs have no legislation for this.' He taps his fingers on the table. 'How did you enter the country?'

'The normal way,' Dad says.

'On a plane,' I say.

'Our passports were stolen.' Lloyd puts his head in his hands.

'We don't know that,' Dad says.

'We do,' I say.

'It was my fault,' Lloyd moans.

'You did not get replacement papers?' Policeman one looks at Dad.

'No.'

'Why?'

'There wasn't time.' Dad crosses his arms.

'And you have no way of proving who you are?' Policeman two leans in on Lloyd.

Dad throws his arms up. 'It isn't illegal!'

'Why are you here?' They shoot him a look.

'Because of me!' I stamp my foot on the floor. This is all stupid. This could have been avoided with telling the truth. 'I was left on a bench as a baby. Under a copy of the *Aftenposten*. I have it if you want to see it?' They shake their heads. 'And we're here because . . .' I watch the clock tick past . . . 'Because . . .'

'Yes?'

'We're here to find out why! Plus we have the right to speak to a solicitor – everyone has that don't they and we have one.'

Dad and Lloyd look at me.

'We do?'

'Mulki is a human rights lawyer remember.' I picture the note, I run my mind over the paper. 'Her number is 477641 652 906. Not that it matters.'

'It does matter,' Dad says. 'It's great.'

'It doesn't.' I look at the clock. 'It's 10.36,' I say and my shoulders sag. 'We just missed our train. It was the only one there was today.'

It's gone.

And the other catching-the-train me zooms off to meet up with the catching-the-plane me and is standing on my birth island tapping his watch. And the real-life me sits in a little white police-station room with a locked door that doesn't even have a window and slumps on to the table.

Unfairness

We ring Mulki.

Dad does the talking. We stare at him when he comes off the phone.

'So?'

'She says we have to ring the British Embassy to apply for emergency travel documents and get an appointment.'

'Great.'

'In Oslo.'

'I'm not going back to Oslo.' The unfairness bubbles up inside me. 'They can't make us.' I dig my fingernails into my hands. 'We're free to go aren't we? We've proved who we are.'

'Yes.' They nod.

'Was it the hotel man?' I look at the policeman. 'Did he ring you?'

'He has legal obligations.' They raise their shoulders.

I knew it. I knew it was him.

'We can take you back to the hotel.' Policeman one points at the door.

'I'd rather walk,' I say and slam out through it. Dad and Lloyd follow.

'I think you were very inspiring,' Lloyd says.

'Let's get some new tickets north,' Dad says. 'We'll sort the passports on the way home.'

'OK,' I say. 'Thanks.' Now we can just get there.

And we walk through the town, past the shops and up the bank to the railway station and Lloyd tries on a pair of pink discounted ski dungarees, but decides against them.

My phone buzzes in my pocket.

It's Bjorn.

Floyd Partington is an MP. Google it. ☹

I google Floyd Partington.

There's a picture of him with his wife. No kids. Shiny red face.

Freaky smile.

Floyd Partington MP.

I show the phone to Dad. He flinches. 'You never said, Lloyd.'

'I know . . .' Lloyd cradles his ears. 'I try to forget,' he says and rushes into the train station.

Inside it's hot and lovely, like getting in a bath when you've been in the freezer. My cheeks go pink and the heat sucks into my bones.

'Why'd you never say?' I drag Lloyd off the information rack.

'He has so much power.' Lloyd frowns. 'I try to forget.'

Me and Dad look at each other.

We all join the queue and Lloyd plays I spy with himself as no one else feels like it.

'Something beginning with B . . . Big person, correct!'

When we get to the front the attendant shakes her head. 'There are no more trains for today,' she says. We know. 'It will have to be tomorrow I'm afraid.'

I look at Dad. 'I'm not staying in that hotel again.'

'How much please?' Lloyd gets out his cash wedge and puts a note on the counter and another and another until he only has two left.

We zip the tickets in Dad's jacket pocket.

'I don't think we can afford to stay at the hotel anyway.' Lloyd looks at the notes.

Dad looks out the window. 'We can't afford to stay anywhere.'

Shadows

We walk back to the hotel to pick up our cases and hand the keys over to the man. I want to poke them into his eyes. He's talking to the guy in the black leather hat. When they see us they smile.

It makes my stomach go cold.

I look under the hat. The man's eyes are blue and hard.

He shoves his hands into gloves and walks out, his feet clicking on the floor.

I look at Dad and Lloyd but they're not even looking.

The hotel man points at our cases which are already downstairs, behind the desk.

I don't like this.

I don't like the idea that he's been in our room with our things. I stare at him.

'Checkout is at ten.' He shrugs.

'Like you're really busy,' I say under my breath. I wish I could bring all the dead and maimed animals

148

alive from the pictures and the walls to charge at him. A massive dustball of see-how-he-likes-it-ness.

He gives us the key deposit back.

Lloyd holds it up. 'Dinner money!' he says.

My deep-down wobbly feeling BOOMS.

I bulge my eyes at Dad.

We leave and walk back up into town and into the tourist information centre which is open today, and pretend to look at leaflets.

The hat man's face stays in my head.

I've seen him before. Haven't I?

Where?

I'm bad at dates. I'm good at details.

Things I see I don't forget.

I know his face, I know it.

'Just popping out for a moment,' Lloyd says and runs out the shop and is gone for

HOURS.

Me and Dad get through every leaflet and brochure in the rack. There's nothing we don't know about the husky day tours and the *raftingsenteret* (river rafting centre).

149

'Dad.' I pick up a skiing leaflet. 'What are we gonna do without money?'

'We'll survive.'

'Like how?'

'I've got credit cards.' He spins the rack.

We did credit-card interest in maths last year and I know enough about it to know that it is *bad*. You borrow a tenner and pay back a hundred.

Kind of.

We don't even have the tenner.

'Won't you get into debt?'

'Don't worry about it.' He scratches the back of his neck.

I do. I do when he doesn't even have a job to pay it off with.

I look at the packs of people in wetsuits with thumbs up in blue inflatable boats. Kids standing on the back of dog sleds. The huskies roped together with their thick fur and tongues sticking out like the ones we saw. Only in snow.

Deep, deep snow.

Dad looks over my shoulder. 'I wish we could do that.'

I look at the prices. 'I know.'

We sit down on a bench with a reindeer hide on.

Lloyd comes back in and his eyes are bright and shiny.

'Where've you been?'

'It's a secret,' he says.

'I don't like secrets.'

'You'll like this one,' he says and we are released into the street.

Pod

'Let go eat!' Lloyd says and we find a cafe and sit in a corner booth and look at the menu with thick plastic pages and order fish burgers and *fiske suppe*. The waiter nods and comes back with plates up both arms.

I squeeze ketchup on to my burger and let the juice dribble down my chin. It's kind of a fishcake but salty and juicy and solid and contains no mash or breadcrumbs at all.

I would record the sound of:

> *sometimes heaven is a hot fish burger*
> *(a knives-and-forks clanking,*
> *busy, busy, sort of sound).*

But I am way too hungry. I think about debt. When people get into debt they lose their houses. Don't they? I saw that on TV. I think about Aunty Ima.

'We could sleep at the station,' I say. 'It's warm and there's benches and it'll have to be open 'cos trains come and go all night.'

'It's not a bad plan.' Dad dips his chips in some ketchup.

'It's the only plan.' I wipe my wrist with my napkin to stop juice going down my sleeve.

After dinner we sit in a bar with glasses of water and watch football on TV. Everyone in here is crazy for Newcastle United. They score and the bar goes nuts.

We go back up to the station and try to squish up in the corner and lie down on the slatted benches. I wouldn't describe it as comfortable. I use my jacket as a blanket and my case as a pillow and try to look like we're gonna get up and get a train any second. I guess we need to get used to uncomfortable.

I think about ringing the address.

One night won't make a difference.

'Cept now it isn't one, it's two.

There's no way I can do it here.

I have to be alone.

'Dad.'

'Yeah.'

153

'I'm sorry this isn't nice,' I say.

'It kind of is,' he says. 'It's kind of like camping.'

'In a pod,' Lloyd says. 'Like dolphins. Or campers.'

And we all pretend we're in a fancy camping pod and I guess I get to sleep at some point 'cos when I wake up Lloyd isn't there.

Head Hunter

The moon lights up the waiting room. It's totally empty (except for Dad and me).

I look out the window. The sky is blue-black and twinkly. The cars are still and shiny.

I look at the bench. Lloyd's rucksack has gone. His case is still there.

Lloyd would never leave his apples.

My heart starts thumping.

Has Floyd got him?

How?

I plug my brain in. It feels spinny, like it needs a recharge.

If Floyd snatched Lloyd he would have yelled.

He would have woken us up. Wouldn't he?

And people would've seen it.

Someone.

Somebody would have noticed.

I can't breathe in here. The air is too hot. I need to get out.

I stand up. Slowly.

Dad doesn't move.

I creep over to the door and go outside.

The street is silent, like someone sucked up all the sound with a vacuum.

I put my hands under my armpits to keep them warm and watch my breath smoke.

I should wake Dad. Should I? Shouldn't I? We should get the police.

I don't want to go back there again. Lloyd didn't have ID, now he's missing in mysterious circumstances. It's too complicated.

I walk over to the railing and look out over the town. It twinkles in the moonlight. Mountains lurch round the sides. Houses huddle in the middle. The sky fades from midnight blue to black. Strange things hide in pretty places sometimes.

I think about the leather-hat man.

Getting off the train.

Staying down our corridor.

Smiling with the hotel man.

I think of Floyd Partington MP's shiny red face.

If he isn't Floyd, who is he?

Was it him?

I see a dark shape, running, huddled over and strange, coming this way.

I duck down under the railing and press my back against the wall.

Crunch

      Crunch

           Crunch.

The feet stop.

Someone puts their hand on my shoulder.

I freeze.

'Found you!' he says.

Moon Flashes

I kick out, hard.

'OW!' The dark huddle starts hopping.

I get up. My feet slip in the ice, but I run. I run down the street into the light.

My feet crunch in the frost and grit.

I slip and grab a lamp post. 'Stop!' The huddle runs after me. 'Wait!'

I skid on to my backside and slide down the hill. It's steep. I slam into the curb. The pain stings my bones.

I feel a hand on my arm. I look up. The moon flashes on the face in the hood.

I pull back from the hard blue eyes.

But they're not there.

There's no hat either.

'Lloyd?'

The surprise of seeing him makes me laugh and I shove my sleeve into my mouth as making noise out here in the silence seems wrong.

I push myself up. 'I thought you were dead, or knocked out, or ...'

'No,' he raises his arms. 'I'm perfectly alive. I sold Uncle Albert's emerald earrings for extra funds,' he says and holds up a new wedge of cash.

'In the middle of the night?'

'It was a long walk to the private buyer's house.' He sits next to me. 'We got talking and he had a very decent bottle of port.'

'How?'

'It's quite easy to import, it's just a little pricey.'

'How did you sell them?'

He holds up his phone. 'Like this!' He shows me the eBay buy-it-now page. 'I offered free personal delivery,' he says and rubs his leg where I kicked it.

'Sorry. I thought you were the hat man.'

'Who?'

'It doesn't matter. Will Uncle Albert miss his earrings?'

'This journey is too important, Elvis.' He looks super serious. 'Floyd will not win,' he says. 'He must not win.'

'You sold the rifle, how else will he win?'

'He wants us to give up.'

159

I think about *Top 10 Ways To Tell If Someone Is Lying*.

1 – Repeating the question.

2 – Sweating.

3 – Smiling.

4 – Avoiding eye contact.

Lloyd looks right at me. I believe him.

I think of us being hunted by Floyd.

Lloyd's head being mounted on a wall like the animal heads at the hotel.

I think about unfairness. I feel a bit bold in the dark. 'Lloyd.'

'Yes.'

'I feel very awake. Do you feel very awake?'

He puts his head from side to side and weighs up his awakeness. 'I'm fifty-five per cent awake,' he says.

'Good. We need to go to the hotel.'

'Yes, their beds are much more comfortable.'

'No,' I say. 'I've got an idea.'

Revenge and Fairness

We walk to the hotel down the middle of the road because we can and there is nothing around to squash us. And I record the sound of:

feeling bold in the middle of the night
(a footsteps-in-gravel, whispering,
expectant sort of sound).

'What is the plan exactly?' Lloyd rubs his ears.

'Revenge and fairness.'

'Excellent.' He nods.

'All those dead animals' pictures and heads are wrong. And that man made us miss our train. He's mean. If it wasn't for him we'd be on my birth island by now.'

We get to the hotel and squat down beside the billboard sign. There is a yellow light on but the reception is empty.

I nudge Lloyd. 'You go in. If he comes out, say

you forgot something. If he doesn't come out, wave at me, OK?'

'Can't you forget something?'

'No. I stared at him, he'll remember me. And kids don't go in hotels in the middle of the night.'

'I forgot my nail clippers,' he says and stands up.

'Excellent.' I keep squatting.

Lloyd goes in with bendy knees. The door swings shut with a

SWOOSH

CLINK.

He doesn't come out. He folds himself over the desk, looks both ways and waves.

I go in.

'What are we going to do?' Lloyd is whispering under the desk.

'This,' I whisper back and we creep into the hotel man's office. It has shelves full of folders and papers, a phone, a decanter of whisky and a photo of the man with a dead deer slung round his shoulders.

I take off my shoes for quietness and run into the dining room and stick one behind the door so it doesn't bang shut and get a salt cellar and run back and pour it in the whisky decanter.

I pass it to Lloyd. 'Shake it.'

He shakes it. I shake it.

'There.'

'Right.'

'Good.'

I picture the man spitting it out all over the papers.

'It doesn't say anything about our thoughts on animal cruelty though does it.' I take a biro off the desk and a wedge of paper out of the printer. I pass Lloyd the heavy-duty Sellotape dispenser. 'Bring this.'

We creep into the dining room and I stand on a chair and I draw a speech bubble coming out of one of the deer's heads on the paper with a biro. It looks weedy.

'Use this.' Lloyd chucks me a pen. 'I always have my Sharpies,' he says and together we draw speech bubbles and write messages from the animals and stick them on with tape:

MY LIFE WAS NOT FOR YOU TO TAKE

and

I LOOK BETTER ALIVE

and

DOWN WITH DEATH ORNAMENTS

As we get a bit tired they get a bit surreal:

GIVE ME A GUN TOO NEXT TIME AND MAKE IT FAIR

and

YOU ONLY PUT ME UP AS YOUR HEAD IS SO UGLY

and

I WILL HAUNT YOU WITH MY EYES
AND THEY WILL FOLLOW YOU ALL AROUND THE
   ROOM
EVEN WHEN YOU TURN AROUND
YOU WILL NEVER ESCAPE ME!

The paper bubbles glow in the moonlight.
I look at the wall of protest. It looks great.

I look at my arms on the walls. The way they make shadows.

I make a tortoise. Kind of.

I pull back and make a deer head by Lloyd's face. He jumps and nearly falls off the chair.

My hand is small. The deer head's massive.

I think about shadows.

Shadows freak you from a distance. Made by someone else.

Someone you can't see. I chase Lloyd with the deer head. It's easy. He doesn't even notice.

Shadows can follow you around.

I think about walking out of this room with the policemen.

Walking back in and seeing the leather-hat man.

His face pings into my brain.

And multiplies.

Images come into focus and merge.

I know who he is.

Run!

He's been everywhere. So often I didn't even notice.

The man with the budgie at the airport.

The one taking a photo of a pigeon on the bus.

The 'after you' man in the newsagent.

He just blended.

He was the perfect shadow.

He was the shadow man.

He's Floyd's shadow.

He's working for Floyd.

'Floyd's hired a detective to follow us.' I jump down off my chair. 'Why would he do that?' I walk over.

'I don't know.' Lloyd looks down and tries to unstick his fingers from the Sellotape dispenser. 'I have no idea.'

I don't believe him.

'The only way to beat him is to tell me.'

'No.'

'Please.' I go closer.

'I can't.' Lloyd drops the dispenser. It crashes to the floor.

We freeze.

There's footsteps upstairs. Great. I take my shoe out the door and slip it on.

It swooshes shut.

We scuttle to the edge of the room and lean up against the wall.

Lloyd's hand crawls over and holds on to mine.

The footsteps come downstairs.

A light goes on in the lobby.

Someone pushes the door open. We pull in flat. I shut my eyes in case they reflect.

And freeze.

The eyes look around in the dark like stealth lasers.

Sometimes the best form of defence is attack. Right?

Right. I run at the door screaming. There's no leather hat. It isn't the shadow. It's the hotel man. I bounce off his stomach, switch the lobby lights off with one hand and pull Lloyd along with the other and steam up the stairs.

I drag him up one floor.

The lights go back on. I flick them off on the landing.

Second floor.

The lights flick back on.

'You do the lights,' I whisper at Lloyd. 'And when he comes, run!'

Lloyd stays on the landing and flicks the light on and off and on and off like a strobe. I put my hand over my eyes and look through my fingers to find room fifty-two.

I bang on the door. 'Open up!' The shadow man better be in there. 'Open up! I've got a message from Floyd,' I yell!

I hear Lloyd shriek and fumble along the corridor. 'He's coming,' he says. 'He's coming.'

I try the handle. The door clicks and uncatches. We fall into room fifty-two and I lock it shut with the switch behind us.

Remington to the Rescue

The room is dark. And silent.

I flick the light on. It blinds us.

The hotel man pushes against the door and yells, 'I'll ring the police!'

I look around. The bed is made. The window is open.

The curtain blows in the breeze.

He leans in and hisses. 'I'll have you deported. I know who you are,' he says. 'I know your little secret.'

So shadow man lied about us? Like how?

I punch the door and bounce his head off the other side.

Lloyd pulls the dresser and I push and we shove it under the handle and block the doorway.

There's a piece of paper on the bed. I pick it up. It's my birth address. I didn't even know it had gone. I tap my jacket. The zip's still done up. But my compass has gone too.

So he's a pickpocket. A spy and a pickpocket.

I turn the paper over.

Thanks, it says on the back. *Most Helpful!*

'Do you not think I have a spare key?' the hotel man says. 'Idiots.' And stomps off downstairs to get it.

I look at the window.

'We've got to jump, Lloyd. If he can do it. So can we.' I run over and look out. Two floors up. How is it possible?

Lloyd runs behind me, his hands tucked up under his armpits. I climb up on to the ledge. I hear the man's feet on the stairs.

'What's going on?' Another door opens.

'Get back in your room!'

I grab for the drainpipe with one hand and hold tight to the window frame with the other. It reaches, my other hand gently lets go and I make a jump over, but it doesn't catch and I slip and fall scraping my hand down the metal and my knees off the bricks all the way to the bottom and go over on my ankle. Lloyd lands next to me with a bounce.

We hear the hotel man yelling upstairs.

I try to stand and get a sharp pain all the way up me. 'Lloyd,' I hiss-whisper. 'I can't walk.'

'Remington to the rescue!' he says and puts his arms out behind and I fling mine round his neck and we bounce off up the hill like a giant preying mantis with an ant on its back.

'Remington?' My teeth jangle.

'It was my superhero nickname.' He strides onward. 'Remington Sword.'

'In the castle?'

'Yes in the castle,' he says. 'I got great at drainpipes.'

We zoom up the hill.

And the blue-black swallows us up.

And I am glad Lloyd and his long bendy legs are in my life.

And I wonder if animal cruelty would have been something I would have ever thought about if he wasn't?

Connections

Lloyd settles me down on the floor by the station door. I hop on my good foot and use his elbow as a crutch back into the waiting room.

'What if he comes in here for us?' I whisper.

'He won't.'

'How?'

'I'll stay awake all night,' Lloyd says and picks me up and plops me down on the bench. 'With mind maths!'

I put my bad foot up on my rucksack and when I wake up I have red slat lines on my good leg from lying in one place and not moving.

Dad stretches and says, 'Slept like a log.'

Lloyd's head bobs with his eyes open. He scratches his chin and says, 'Two hundred and eight sevens are one thousand four hundred and fifty-six.'

A woman with a carrier bag stares at him and I say, 'Hmmn, bad late trains,' and look at my watch like we missed one.

Lloyd says, 'I sold Uncle Albert's emerald earnings last night. Amongst other things.'

He winks at me and hands me and Dad a cash wedge each. 'Just in case,' he says.

'In case of what?' I rub my leg and try to stand on it. It works. Just.

Dad strokes his goalpost moustache and tries to hand the money back. 'I can't take it,' he says.

'No.' Lloyd backs off. 'Your friendship is my sacred jewel,' he says and the train pulls in before we can argue.

I hobble on Lloyd's elbow on to the platform and we get on and shove the cases in the rack and walk along to the buffet car and when the waiter says, 'Can I help you?' This time I say, '*Ja tak*,' and order Dad and Lloyd waffles and coffee with my cash wedge. I get Lloyd three coffees. I don't have coffee so I have waffles with waffles and we all have them hot with raspberry jam and sour cream which is so thick it spreads.

It is the

BEST

breakfast ever.

And I record the sound of:

buying things for other people tastes nice
(a silent happy-eating, rail-track-
bumping kind of sound).

I imagine the man at the hotel's face when he comes downstairs.

And I look around and wonder where the shadow man is now?

'Dad.' I lick the last bit of jam off my fingers. 'We had a bit of an incident.'

Lloyd falls asleep on the buffet car table and I tell Dad everything.

His face goes pale.

'It doesn't make any difference,' I say. 'Now we have the advantage.'

Dad rubs his head and pulls his hair. 'How?'

'We have knowledge,' I say. 'We know how Floyd's following us. We know he knows it too. We know what the shadow detective looks like.' I tap my fingers on the table. 'Knowledge is power.'

'I want the compass back,' Dad says and looks livid.

'Me too,' I say. 'Me too.'

We travel all day and watch hills and fjords and

lush green fields bouncing along out of the window like it's a screen. Lloyd wakes up after lunch and I buy us all Dumle ice creams with thick chocolate tops and caramel middles and we play hangman. I look at Lloyd's writing all neat and curled and flicky.

I look at the Ks.

'How do you write like that?'

'We had a tutor.'

'In the castle?' He nods.

'Mrs Phipps,' he says. 'I wish we'd gone to normal school.'

I think he'd have been eaten alive in *normal school* and tuck that fact into my mind.

There are three of them then.

Three possible people with flicky Ks.

Lloyd, Floyd and Mrs Phipps.

Three people could have written those notes.

The sun stretches out over the water. Tucks itself behind trees. Jumps out of rocks. I see a massive boulder in someone's garden in the middle of a fence. I think if rocks could talk they'd say, 'I'm here, deal with it. Move your fence.'

I think about things in the way.

Bjorn was right.

We are going to the same place.

Floyd was following us.

Now he's got my address.

I have to ring it.

It's been three days already.

I stick my phone up my sleeve and wobble off to the toilet.

Magic Magic Siri

I shut the seat and sit down. The walls are green leaves to look like a forest. Nice.

There's no window. Not nice.

I feel a bit claustrophobic.

The wheels thunder under. The hinges squeak and rattle.

I look down and reach out for the magic hand of the universe.

'Hey, Siri.'

'Hey, Elvis.'

'You have a big brain.'

'Who me?'

'Yes.'

'I thought so.'

'I need you to find a phone number.'

'What kind of businesses are you looking for?'

'I need you to find the phone number for Skriva, Norway.'

'Here's what I found for screamo no way.'

'Find phone number for Skriva, 8320 Norway.'

'Here's what I found on the web for scroll that no way. Have a look.'

'Find phone number for

S

K

R

I

V

A

Norway.'

'I found three places named SKRIVA. Tap the one you are looking for.'

All it comes up with is a farm.

And two places that aren't anywhere near.

'Stupid Siri,' I yell at the phone.

'That's not nice.'

I can't ring without a number.

I put my phone back in my pocket and smack my head on the handrail.

The train lurches to a stop.

Hmmmn

It's a normal train break. We swap platforms – down through tunnel steps, up other steps, through a waiting room portal and on to the new train.

It's totally different inside.

We squeeze the cases down the corridor with locked doors on one side and windows on the other and queue up to get a key card off a guard in the buffet carriage.

I use my fast eyes to look down the names list. Is Floyd on?

Did the shadow man follow us here?

The guard sees me looking. She closes the folder and hands us the key.

I only got as far as the Ds.

Not the Ps.

I kick my foot into the table. Pain shoots up my leg.

She ticks our names off a list and we squeeze back down the corridor again.

A family comes towards us from the other end. Lloyd says, 'Retreat!' We go backwards. They shuffle down into their compartment. I say, 'Attack,' and we go forwards. When someone opens a door no one else can get through.

Lloyd flaps the side seat down next to the window and blocks the aisle.

'Look at this!' he says.

I don't know what it's for. Maybe looking out instead of sleeping?

I slot the key into our door and open it. Inside is a cabin with bunk beds and a washbasin just like the website. 'Surprise!' I say. 'Cept now I don't feel happy. Now I just feel angry. And confused.

Me and Dad are 68/70. Lloyd is next door. He knocks on the wall. I knock back and eat the square chocolates off the pillows.

Lloyd comes in and we sit on Dad's bunk for a while and I flick the light switches – top bunk, lower bunk, sink, reading light – before the train starts to move. I can hear other people banging down the corridor. I wonder who they are.

The train sways off out of the station and we

stare out the window, past the curtains at the world going by:

bright station lights

    grass

        fields.

I need to get back to the names list.

I need to ring the address.

How?

I look out the window at the yellow sky and the red mountains. I look at my watch. 'It's half past nine.'

'It's lighter up north,' Dad says. 'It's the land of the midnight sun.'

'When does it get dark?'

'It doesn't.'

I imagine walking over a mountain at three a.m. that looks like lunchtime.

Weird.

But nice.

Dad goes to the loo and Lloyd leans over and says, 'Elvis. Keep safe.'

'Why?' I say. 'Floyd's after you, not me, Lloyd.'

And Lloyd says, 'Hmmn,' and pats me on the shoulder and leaves.

Boldness

We change into our pyjamas and I get into bed. Dad pulls the ladder down and climbs on to the top bunk. I watch some graffiti flash by on a white wall.

'Will you fall out?' I imagine him landing on the floor like a heavy sausage. BOOM.

'I dunno,' he says and clicks the strap that's a bit like a seat belt and supposed to hold him in.

I lie in bed and wonder what Lloyd was on about?

I need to know if Floyd's on the train.

If he's on it I'll ask him myself.

I listen to the sound of:

feeling bold in the middle of the night.

I was bold once.

I can do it again.

I grab a pencil and two drink mats off the sink and get up.

Dad looks down at me. 'Where are you going?'

'Toilet,' I say and shut the door before he asks anything else.

I can't tell him. If I do he'll say, *DON'T. It's dangerous. Leave it.*

But I can't.

I walk down to the buffet car in my socks. It's kind of weird in pyjamas. My feet bounce over the plastic where the carriages join together. The buttons make the doors open and hiss. They're like giant yellow hissing wine gums. A door closes behind me. A door opens in front.

I hold myself up on the wall with my arm and shuffle my bad leg and keep going.

I smell the buffet car before I see it. It smells of heat and spice and sausages. The waiter is wiping the ketchup bottle with a blue cloth. 'We are closing in ten minutes,' he says.

'I need to see the guard,' I say.

'Why?'

I cross my fingers up my sleeves. 'I lost my dad. I need to see the compartment list so I can find the right room and get back in.'

The waiter hands over the clipboard off the shelf

behind him and goes back to the ketchup. I run my finger down the plastic-covered page.

```
Pedersen, Knut
Philiips, Jorn
Partington, Floyd
```

My heart skips.

The guard walks through the door and stares at me. 'What do you want?' she says.

'Got it,' I say and snap it shut. 'Thanks.' I pass it to the waiter and walk fast out the door and don't look back.

It hisses shut behind me.

I go down the corridor past the compartments, bouncing my hands off the walls. I see the mountains flicking by. I see a herd of deer run. Their white bums bounce. I wonder why natural selection has selected that? It makes them so easy to kill. It seems unfair. It's like sticking a target on their butt. I feel like a target in my pyjamas.

I put my ear to his door and listen.

It's silent.

I wonder if he's in.

'JUST SHOOT THE BUGGERS,' a voice says.
'THEY'RE ONLY BADGERS FOR GOD'S
SAKE.' It's definitely Floyd.

I take out a drink mat. The writing space is small.
But possible.

I write:

What do you want?

And slide it under the door.
The mat slips through like a hot knife in butter.
I wait.
It slides back out, like underdone toast.

Who are you?

I write:

Elvis

and slide it back.
There's a laugh behind the door. Not a nice one.
For a minute I think he might open it. I run up
the corridor in my silent socks and into a man with

185

a towel on and a toothbrush. *'Beklager,'* he says and walks by. The drink mat slips out of Floyd's door. The man walks past and his wet foot stands on it. It sticks. I watch it going up and down, up and down like a leaf on a car tyre. I panic. I think the writing will get smudged off.

I run after the man, squatting like a frog person, hoping it will drop off. It doesn't.

He gets his key out. I tap him on the shoulder.

'You trod on something,' I say and rip it off his foot and hobble off. I skid down the corridor and stop by the window and hold it in the light.

It isn't too smudged.

I can still read it.

It's just one word:

Justice

Help?

I go back to our compartment and knock.

'Who is it?' Dad says.

'Me.'

There's a stretching noise as Dad leans over to open the door and I go in. 'You were gone a long time. You all right?'

'Fine,' I say. My blood is bouncing.

'You sure?'

'Yeah.' I flop into bed. Justice? It's something. But nothing.

It could mean anything.

Dad sits up and folds his head over the bed. 'Elvis.'

'Hmmn,'

'Don't do anything stupid.'

'Like what?' I rub my ankle. 'Why does Floyd care about me, Dad? Why is he bothered?'

'I don't know.' Dad looks really serious.

'It feels like a race.' I flick the sink light on and off.

'Look.' He puts his book down. 'Don't get your hopes up.'

'About what?'

'About tomorrow. About your parents. You might find something you don't like.'

'People don't leave babies for no reason.' I pick my fingers. Everyone knows that much.

'I want to make sure you know what you're getting into.'

'Do you?' I tilt my head up.

He pulls back. 'How would I?'

I look at him.

Everyone feels suspicious.

Even Dad?

He sighs. 'Everyone deserves to know where they've come from,' he says. 'I wanted you to see the place. You deserve that much. Places stay. People come and go. People are unpredictable.'

I look out the window and wonder if this is a journey I've made before another time. Inside somebody else. *Her*. When her sounds were all I had. Before I was born into silence and taken away.

The train squeaks and groans.

And I think about the world and me shuttling through it in a train capsule like blood to a heart.

And I think about my bedroom, empty, without me in it.

I think about the truth.

Getting closer and closer.

I think about justice.

Justice means getting what's right and what's fair and not being left in the dark. Doesn't it?

What's the difference between justice and revenge?

I don't want to want the same thing as Floyd.

But I do. Don't I?

I think about Bjorn. *If I were you I'd ring it.*

I think about Dad. *You might find something you don't like.*

Are they there or not?

I get out of bed again.

If I can face Floyd, I can do anything. Can't I?

I just need a little help.

Shadow Hands

I get my phone out and look at the list of numbers
Siri came up with.

They're useless.

The bed shakes.

My bones rattle.

My heart rattles.

I think of the train like a wolf. Running. Running.
Like a husky with a sled.

Dragging us along.

I listen to the clacks on the tracks.

Go on

        Go on

          Go on.

I look at the back of my hand. At the blue biro
smear.

Maybe I need people, not machines.

I text Bjorn. And cross my fingers, hoping he's
about.

You there?

We didn't lose Floyd.

He doubled. He hired a detective.

I need some help.

I need to find the phone number.

Do It!

I send Bjorn the address and lie in bed, clutching the phone.

When I wake up the train has stopped. I open the door and see people banging down the corridor in their pyjamas.

I look at the screen to see if Bjorn's had a breakthrough yet.

Nothing.

'The train will depart in fifteen minutes,' the announcement says.

I knock on Lloyd's door. He is fully dressed. 'Me and Owen had an interesting conversation about cheese,' he says and points to the man in his compartment. The man sticks his head out and waves.

Dad just stretches and rubs his eyes like a vampire.

We put clothes on and Dad swears at the case, which won't shut, and we squeeze along the corridor with everyone else and get off into a station made of glass.

It feels like being in a fishbowl full of light. Other people get off the train and trail away. This place feels slow and easy. Suitcases grumble over the concrete.

I pull us into the 7-Eleven behind the magazine racks and look for Floyd.

He knows we're here now.

I found out nothing and gave everything away.

Lloyd picks up *Big Eye* magazine. 'Look at the eyes!' he says and holds it in front of our faces.

I buy us hot chocolate and cinnamon buns and *Melkesjokolade* with my cash. Under the wrapper all the chocolate bars are like little medieval cities. 'Takes years for the elves to carve these out,' Dad says and eats his in two bites and gets an espresso. We turn round the postcard stand and look at postcards of the north.

Mountains like teeth.

Snow.

Racks of fish on washing lines.

'The north is so special!' A woman walks past and smiles.

I look outside.

There is no sign of Floyd. Or the shadow.

193

Yet.

We run over the concourse and into a car-hire shop and Dad hires a Peugeot 306 with his cash wedge.

BING.

My phone flashes with two big thumbs up.

And the number.

Bjorn's a genius.

I text him.

You sure?

Dad sorts the forms. Without the passports it takes ages.

I sneak out the front door and round the back.

I look around and press my back against the wall and click the number.

It rings.

A long weird beep.

BEEEEEP

I look at Dad through the window, signing the yellow papers.

BEEEEEP

It stops. A woman answers.

'*Hei hei,*' she says.

My chest is so tight I can't breathe.

I have to speak.

I have to say something.

'Hello,' I say.

'Hello?' she says.

I feel our brains connecting through wires across space like hands rushing through the air.

Tapping her on the shoulder.

Her.

It's her.

Is it?

I'm coming, I think.

Don't let Floyd in, I want to say.

But the silence coils around us.

And chokes me.

I shrink back.

'Who is this? You must stop! Stop doing this!' she says and hangs up.

Brothers

I run back into the shop and pour a cup of water with the little handle on the water cooler like in a bar. The drips run away into the overspill. I drink it and breathe.

I think of her voice.

Who is this? You must stop! Stop doing this!

Did someone ring before?

Who?

Floyd?

He got the address off me.

Lloyd?

He took a photograph of it on the bus.

How would they even get the number? I couldn't do it without Bjorn.

Dad?

He had the address all along.

Why would he call and not say anything?

'Coming?' Dad looks over his shoulder like I'd never gone.

I gulp the water and nod.

We go round the back and into the car. It's blue and smells of headaches.

We load our stuff into the boot and drive off. We go really slowly and stop at traffic lights.

And I say, 'Floyd was on the train last night,' to see if they knew.

Lloyd bristles. 'How do you know?'

'I saw his name on the passenger list.'

Dad brakes hard at the lights. 'When's it gonna end, Lloyd?'

I look at Dad and Lloyd for signs of lying.

I don't think either of them are.

They didn't know.

The light goes green.

Lloyd says, 'You can do forty here.'

And Dad says, 'I am doing forty.'

And Lloyd says, 'It's this way isn't it?'

And Dad says, 'NO.'

And Lloyd says, 'There's no need to say it like that.'

And Dad says, 'I didn't say it like anything.'

I wind my window down and look out the back

for anything suspicious. We leave the town and head out through green-field blur.

The water hits my bladder and we stop to wee in a bush next to a waterfall which gushes out of the rock like blood from a giant's arm that's been cut off. It crushes out the sounds of everything else, grinding them up on the rocks with its water fists. I record:

power

(a hissing – rushing – sound).

We get back in the car. It is a bubble of breathing and silence. Dad plays 'What is Normal?' by the Lovely Eggs and we drive on, over a hill and round a bend. I look out and see a road that goes into the sea for miles. It rises up on concrete pillars, over bridge arcs, past red barns and fishing huts and rocks like a Scalextric on water. The waves froth white and blue. The sky opens out. Gulls shriek and squeal. I get out my phone and wind down the window to make a video.

I pan front.

I pan behind.

There's a red Alpha Romeo Spider tailing us. With a flat cap behind the wheel. A weaselly face under the flat cap.

'Dad.'

'Yeah.'

'Floyd alert,' I say and point out the back.

Lloyd looks like he's gonna be sick.

Dad grips the wheel. 'Right,' he says and steps on the accelerator and we lurch off.

Go, Peugeot 306, go.

We are the Floyd, Lloyd and Us challenge.

Bring it on.

I've never seen Dad rally drive. He's actually really good.

Floyd weaves to the right. He sneers.

Peugeot against Alpha. Alpha against Peugeot. A lion against a spider. A weasel against wild beasts. We roar. The brakes squeal.

We screech over the first bridge. And scream round the corner. My phone skids across the back seat and I catch it before it falls off.

Floyd follows. The spider grips the road. Close. The lion revs and smells of burning.

We turn left around a white barn, right on to

an island. We island skim like a stone over the sea. I grip the headrest to protect my elbows.

I stick my head out. The air blasts past and shoves into my mouth. It's great.

Floyd sticks an arm out of his window with an air rifle. This is not great.

Dad yells, 'Get yer head in.'

Floyd shoots. DING. It pings off a rock. Again. DING. It just misses the hubcap. We nearly lost a tyre.

'How is he shooting?' I see Dad's eyes in the rear-view mirror.

'He's using one hand.'

Lloyd ducks down on to the floor and says in a quiet voice, 'I am as strong as you, Floyd. I am a strong confident man.'

We hit a straight bit of road. Floyd has two hands now. His feet are on the pedals. Nothing on the wheel. He has us in his sights.

He aims lower. PING. It stotts off the road railing. Dad swerves right.

A Nissan Leaf honks round the bend.

'He's going for the tyres,' I yell. 'It's the only way to stop us.'

The road climbs up to a bridge, the bridge stilts rise up over the water, heading for the land. He can't miss this. He grins. His ferret face is red. His eyes twinkle.

Dad slams on the brakes. I bounce off the seat in front.

'What are you doing?'

'I'm not running from him.' Dad reverses. Full force.

We screech on the tarmac.

'We're going to die!' Lloyd yells.

The world slows into slo-mo.

Dad doesn't back down.

Floyd doesn't back off.

I have to do something.

I must do something. My rucksack skids across the floor.

I put my arm out the window. 'You want justice. Take some justice,' I yell, and pull my birth newspaper out and chuck it.

It flies through the air like a paper bird.

Into the sky and down.

Down down down.

On to the Spider's windscreen.

It opens its wings and lands, covering everything. Floyd swerves.

BOOM.

Dad slams on the brakes. I look behind.

Floyd's crashed into the side railing. His airbag is out and his head is in it. Like a raspberry in a marshmallow. Steam's coming out of the engine. There's a dent in the bonnet.

'Nice shot.' Dad high-fives me backwards and switches the gears into accelerate.

Lloyd crawls out from the footwell and looks behind in the wing mirror.

'I hope he's OK,' he says and looks sad.

'He wanted to shoot us.' I wind my window up. 'Why do you care?'

'He's still my big brother,' he says.

And I wonder about brothers.

And I wonder if I have one that I don't know about. And if he's nice.

He would be nice, wouldn't he? What if he's with *them* and I'm not. What if there's lots of them. Brothers, sisters, altogether. What if they're a big happy family without me?

What if he's like Floyd?

What if?

What if?

What if?

And I think about how in films, families are always really nice and get on and go out for pizza and how life isn't really like that at all.

Flat

'Next stop the ferry,' Dad says and zooms off.

Lloyd's eyes sparkle. 'We'll get there, Elvis!' He punches the air with both hands. 'We'll get there.'

'Well done on the paper,' Dad says. 'Where'd you find that?'

'It was my birth paper.'

Dad stops the car. 'Seriously?'

A white pickup goes by and honks.

He puts the hazard lights on.

The car is silent.

'That was a piece of you,' Lloyd says.

'Well at least we're not dead,' I say. 'Or they'd be lots of pieces of me.' I look out the window. 'And I don't need it do I? This afternoon we'll meet them and I'll know.'

Dad gives Lloyd a look.

'Whatever happens,' I say, 'it isn't who I am any more. I don't need it. OK.'

'OK,' Dad says and blows out.

I tuck my feet up on the seat. 'Can we just get going please?'

'Sure.' Dad bulges his eyes and drives off and we stop after a bit at *Statoil* (petrol station) to get sandwiches. Me and Lloyd open the bakery drawers. The lids lift when you pull them open and the smell comes out. Lloyd opens and closes the drawers till the attendant stops him. I get a hot pizza slice and *Potetgull* crisps.

I think that the shadow is nowhere. Where'd he go?

Sometimes the things you can't see are the scariest.

Lloyd gets out a coconut bun.

'Where's the shadow man gone?' I look at him.

He drops the bun. 'I don't know, Elvis.' He swallows. 'I don't know.'

When we get back to the car, it's slumped on one side. My side. I put my slice on the roof and squat down. Dad just stares at it, sandwich in one hand, coffee in the other. 'Slow flat,' he says. 'The pellet must have stuck.'

I run my finger over the hot black rubber. 'Unless someone knifed it.' I point at a slit leaking air.

'Change it, George, change it!' Lloyd jumps up and down.

'I've never changed a tyre,' Dad says.

I look at my watch. 'The ferry leaves in two hours.' I wipe my hands on my jeans. 'We can google it.'

'We have to!' Lloyd puts his hand to his head. 'We have to!'

'Yeah.' Dad sighs. 'But I can't fix it fast enough.'

'We're at a garage.' I point at the sign. 'They can fix it.'

'That's actually a really good idea,' Dad says and goes in. I watch them talking through the window. Lloyd paces back and forth. Dad comes out shaking his head. 'I'm sorry,' he says and puts a hand on my shoulder. 'They only do the selling. They're not allowed to leave the till. Regulations.' He shrugs. 'We're stuck for tonight. We'll never make it.'

'No!' Lloyd yells. 'This can't be happening!'

'Chill out, Lloyd.' I try to put a hand on his arm.

'How can I?' he spits.

'Whoa!' Dad holds up his hands like Lloyd's a wild horse.

Lloyd yells and swings his bread-roll bag up and

down. 'What if he gets there first? What if he gets there first?' Lloyd pales. 'We could get a helicopter. We could get a new car. We could steal a car.'

He starts looking around the parking lot.

A car beeps behind us. We're blocking the pumps.

'We're not stealing a car,' Dad says.

The car behind beeps again and yells something I don't get. Dad waves his hand like, *Yes yes we're going.* 'It's just one more day. What difference does it make?'

'All the difference in the world.' Lloyd slumps on to the ground.

I stand over him. 'Why, Lloyd?'

'Floyd doesn't want you to meet your mother, Elvis,' he says.

'Why not?'

'I can't say. I can't say!' He throws up his arms and bursts into tears and Dad scoops him up under both arms and shoves him into the back seat.

Close

Dad drives off into the parking space.

I turn round and look at Lloyd.

It was him who rang. It must have been him. Was it?

'You rang the house. It was you!'

Dad looks totally confused.

'Yes.' Lloyd hangs his head. 'It was me.

'Did you speak to her?'

'No.' He shakes his head.

'Who?' Dad holds his hands up.

'Lloyd rang my birth address.'

'So did you.' Lloyd points at me. 'I wanted to make sure Floyd wasn't there. I wanted to make sure Floyd hadn't got there first.'

'Why didn't you speak to her?'

'She wouldn't.'

'Why not?' I screw my eyes up.

'She only wants to speak to *you*.'

'You said no more secrets! How can I trust you if you don't tell me the truth?'

'Sometimes the truth is hard.' Dad sighs.

'Like what?' I turn on him. 'What do you know?'

'I don't want you to get hurt.'

'You deserve better ...' Lloyd puts his hands over his eyes.

'Is that where you went?' Dad looks at me. 'On the train. You went to ring the address?'

'No, on the train I went to find Floyd.'

'Great.' Dad taps the steering wheel and rubs his hair. 'So you keep secrets too then yeah? That's how secrets are. Complicated.'

I tuck my hands in my armpits. 'At least mine are about me. They're not about anyone else.' I look at Lloyd. I think about the Ks. 'Is it Mrs Phipps?'

'Who's that?' Dad spins round.

Lloyd looks surprised. 'No.'

'Why doesn't he want me to meet my mother,' I say. 'It doesn't make sense.'

'It's news to me,' Dad says. He looks at Lloyd. 'And we're going, whatever Floyd says.' He takes a swig of coffee. 'But not tonight.' He hands me the phone. 'You wanna pick somewhere?' I click the app open. 'Just make it close.' He takes a bite out of his sandwich. 'And be quick before the tyre hits the ground and I have to drive it on the rims.'

Magic Hands

I pick Tiny's Retreat 'cos it has a cool dog and we drive there in silence.

Lloyd's hunched in a ball in the back seat and won't speak.

I eat the pizza and think.

Floyd wants to get there first.

Bjorn was right.

We're definitely going to the same place.

Why?

Lloyd won't say.

Dad doesn't know.

There's only one person to ask what's going on.

I need to ring back.

I have to ask her.

This time I actually *have* to say something.

We drive on along by the sea, past little bundles of houses stuck in clumps to the edges like shells on rocks.

Slowly.

We go left off the road, roll down through a thick green fir forest. The car bumps and bounces. I slide over the wrong side of the seat and we go out the other side of the woods and into the driveway of a cabin.

'Tiny's Retreat,' Dad says and looks at the sign. The house looks massive and made of wood.

'It's not that tiny.'

'No.' He taps the wheel.

A dog the size of a polar bear trots out to meet us, ears pricked. It puts its paws up on the Peugeot window and looks in, like we're seals under the ice flow. Its eyes are big and blue.

It's bigger than the photo.

We stare back. Dad waves.

A woman comes out and claps her hands and says, 'Tiny. *Nei. Nei*, Tiny,' and he gets down and walks back to the house.

'*Hei hei!*' She waves and we get out.

'I'm Jean,' she says and we shake hands.

'I'm George Lucas, not that George Lucas,' Dad says.

'I'm Elvis. Not that Elvis,' I say.

'I'm Lloyd,' says Lloyd. 'I used to be a Partington

but now I don't really know who I am.' His eyes are watery and red.

'OK.' She smiles. 'This is Tiny,' she says. Tiny barks.

We follow Jean and Tiny into the cabin and take our shoes off.

Outside it is bright red with a veranda all the way around. It has a porch swing and candles hanging down in lanterns. Inside it is white and wooden with rugs and lots of windows and walls full of photos of people up mountains and in canoes with sparklers and eating hot dogs.

We go down into the basement. It's cut into the rocks and looks out on to the lake. We have our own flat with windows that go down to the floor and open out on to a wooden deck with a hammock and a bench with deer painted on it and a beach with a canoe.

We leave our bags and go back up into the kitchen where Jean makes cups of tea and a man with a blue baseball hat comes in through the back door. He kisses Jean and hands her two big fish from behind his back. He wipes his hand on his checked shirt.

She smiles. 'This is Steinar,' Jean says and puts

the fish in the sink and says something to him in Norwegian.

He shakes hands with everyone and Dad says, 'Are you any good with flat tyres?'

And he spreads his arms and says, 'Of course!'

And they go out to fix it.

I go down to the basement. My bed is built into the wall. An old plank of wood comes down from the ceiling and one from the floor. It's like a bed envelope. I post myself in and lie on the sheepskin rug inside.

Jean knocks and comes in with some chocolate cake with squirty cream and sweets on the top. She and Steinar are so smiley and nice.

I put the cake on the table and look out the window at the water.

I get my phone out and listen to:

Power.

I slide my back down the door, using my body to keep it shut.

My heart beats.

I switch the phone on.

I feel hot. My hands sweat.

I press green.

It rings.

>A long beeeeeeeeeeeep
>
>>pause
>
>A long beeeeeeeeeeep
>
>>pause.

Click, she answers.

I say it fast before she can speak.

'It isn't Lloyd, it's Elvis.'

'Elvis . . .' She pauses.

I think I'm freaking her out. That makes two of us.

I hate phones. They don't leave space for gaps. Gaps sound stupid. People need to speak without speaking. Sometimes there's just way too much to say.

'I'm coming.' I try to fill the silence, to keep going. 'Tomorrow.'

'OK.' Her voice is hard to read.

'On the ferry . . .'

'Someone will be there to meet you,' she says and hangs up.

Guessing and Surprises

I sit there for a while. I don't know how long.

Was that her?

Why didn't she say so?

I feel angry.

And stupid that I didn't ask.

Someone will be there to meet you.

That's good isn't it?

Someone walks into the door from the other side.

'OW! ... Elvis.'

'What?'

'Open up.'

Dad is standing there in a wet towel. 'We fixed the car!'

'Cool.'

'Jean's made dinner.' He pulls a T-shirt over his head.

'You all right?'

'Yeah.' I turn away.

'Hey.' He pats my shoulder. 'We're still going.

Tomorrow you get to see where you were born. That's all that matters.' He breathes out. 'Anything else is a bonus. OK?'

'OK.'

He stares at the mountains and sings,

'The hills are alive with the sound of music.'

'Right?' he says. 'Or do you want me to sing it a little louder?' He comes right up to my face.

'OK.' I smile. 'OK.' And we go off into the kitchen to eat meatballs and gravy with potatoes without skin that look like hot eggs and talk about England and fishing and life in the mountains.

'In the winter we dig our way out with a tractor,' Steinar says and ladles thick gravy out of a yellow jug.

After dinner Dad and Lloyd help with the washing-up and me and Jean and Steinar take Tiny swimming in the fjord and throw him sticks. He doesn't like giving them back so we have to keep finding new ones.

'Why are you here in Norway?' Steinar says.

'I was left on a bench as a baby,' I say. 'I'm here to find out why.'

'OK,' he says and snaps a twig in two in his thick hands. Tiny barks his head off. 'So when will you find out?'

'Tomorrow. Tomorrow we go north.'

'The north is so special.' Jean puts her hand on her heart.

'Jean and I could never have children,' Steinar says. 'It was not to happen for us.'

'Oh.' I pick the bark off a stick. 'Sorry,' I say.

He shrugs. 'It is good to know these things. You are not all the time guessing. You get on with your life.'

'Tiny is our baby now.' Jean smiles and Tiny comes out of nowhere and shakes water all over us. They laugh.

Dad comes out and we light a fire to keep away the flies and watch the sun not setting over the water and when I go to bed I lie there thinking about tomorrow and how messed up the world is.

People who want kids can't have them.

People who can don't want them.

They didn't want me.

Didn't they?

I think about what Steinar said:

You are not all the time guessing.
Whatever happens I won't be guessing any more.
Not after tomorrow.
And it doesn't feel weird.
It feels good.

Cold and Empty

I have this dream about a room.

It's cold.

And empty.

And there's a mirror in it.

But I can't see the reflection.

I go closer.

Closer.

And a hand comes out and circles over my face. It stretches and tries to grab me.

I back away. It stretches and stretches. Feeling around. Desperate.

It reaches my chest.

I back into the wall.

And wake up with a shudder.

Belonging

I look at the clock. Four thirty.

I get up and walk into the kitchen.

Tiny's in his basket.

I put my hand out so he can sniff that it's me and feed him some ham out of the fridge so he doesn't bark. He barks for more ham.

His claws click on the floor as he paws them up and down.

Steinar comes in.

He is dressed and rubbing his eyes.

'You big beast, Tiny.' He yawns and pets Tiny's head. 'I am fishing,' he says and smiles. Tiny nuzzles into his leg. 'You are early.' He looks at me. 'I think you are worried about today, yes?'

'I had a weird dream.' I put my fingers deep into Tiny's fur.

'OK!' Steinar says and looks excited. 'Tell me about it!'

He gets a packet out of the cupboard and a pot

of cream out of the fridge. '*Romigrot.*' He taps the packet. 'Norwegian porridge, very special. Let us celebrate this weird dream.'

He gets a pan down and starts making the porridge. 'We heat this till the cream turns to butter,' he says and pours the cream in. 'I am listening.' He stirs.

I tell him about it.

His eyes go big.

'You know, Elvis, in my life I have many dreams also.' He pours the porridge into the bowls and shakes cinnamon on top. It flows into the liquid butter.

'Once my mother was on holiday in America and I have this dream about bridges. A big long white bridge – all the way across the ocean. A mighty bridge.' He makes his arms mighty and I smile. 'She rings the next day and says, *I was on this bridge yesterday* ... and describes to me the exact same bridge. And I say yes, it is exactly the same bridge. How can I know this?' His eyes go big. 'How can I dream this? I don't know, but her thoughts pass into me. She even buys me this.' He points to a fridge magnet with a big white bridge on. 'When Jean cannot have babies too, I know. I have this dream. The room is dark. It is cold and there is no one in. It is very sad. I wake up and say, *Jean, I think the baby is not here.* We go for the scan and the baby is not there any more.'

He looks into his empty bowl.

I think how his dream is kind of like mine.

'But I don't think you are dreaming about babies?' He grins. 'Are you, Elvis? You are not thinking about being a daddy. Not yet! But perhaps you are thinking, *I wonder what my mother will be like, I wonder if she will be there,* yes? Maybe this dream tells you something?'

'Maybe.' I smile. Steinar makes everything seem so normal. Like anything is possible.

'The world is stronger than we know. Your body tells you things.' He puts a fist on his chest. 'Trust your body,' he says. 'Listen to yourself.'

He looks me right in the eye and grins. 'OK!'

'OK.' I nod.

'Good!' Now we must do the washing-up before Jean gets cross and says, "Steinar, where is my porridge?" yes!'

Steiner puts the radio on.

We wash the bowls and spoons and pans.

Tiny gets under our legs.

Dad comes in and yawns. He puts a hand on my shoulder. 'You're early.'

I nod. 'We had *romigrot*.'

'Cool.' Dad squints and makes coffee.

Steinar goes out to fish. I go out too to say goodbye and check over his boat. If he stabbed our tyre, what else is Floyd's shadow gonna do?

We walk past a boat with two men and a baby in a car seat, stuffed in with a life jacket. The baby's eyes are very big and staring.

'*Hei hei*,' they say.

'*Hei hei*,' we say and I check the boat for holes. It seems fine. Steinar pushes it out from the shore till his boots are soaking and I wave until he's a tiny dot in the water.

Dad puts the cases in the car.

Lloyd trails out and slips on to the back seat.

Jean gives me a stick. 'In Norway we say that our lives are like collecting wild strawberries on a straw,' she says. 'The strawberries are the great moments. I hope you find one today.'

We hug and wave.

I get in.

Maybe staying here was a strawberry.

Clink

The car door shuts.

Clunk

The seat belt slots.

Scrape

Tiny's claws slide down the windscreen as he slips off the roof of the car.

He is sitting on the bonnet.

Maybe he doesn't want us to go.

Or maybe it's just nice and warm on the bonnet.

'Down, Tiny. Down!' Jean tries to drag his collar.

He doesn't move. Tiny does not come down.

Dad reverses.

Tiny stays put.

He sits and stares through the glass.

We go over a bump.

He slides off.

We turn round and drive down the drive.

He chases us.

I see his big white polar-bear fluff romping. Paws up and down. Determination in his eyes.

'Here, Tiny! Here!' Jean yells.

Tiny does not come here.

    Engine

        Bark

    Engine.

We drive through the woods.

He looks like a prehistoric beast.

A white streak in green.

Muscle and eyes and paws.

    He runs.

        The engine growls.

        He runs.

We come out of the dark and the woods and crunch in the gravel.

We're at the end of the track.

I hope he won't get squashed. A car buzzes by on the road.

I think he will get squashed.

Tik, Tik, Tik. The indicator pushes us on.

I look out the back window. Tiny stops by the woods and howls.

This is the edge of his territory. He won't go any further. He knows where he belongs.

By this afternoon, so will I.

Don't Look Back

There is no sign of Floyd. Or anyone else. Lloyd keeps rubbing his knuckles and saying, 'He's got there, he's got there first.'

If he was, she would have said on the phone, wouldn't she?

Unless he held a gun to her head?

Unless going there's what he wants us to do?

We stop opposite a car-hire shop.

Dad opens the door. 'There are no cars allowed on the island,' he says. I get out and stare at the big pool of blue with mini islands and boathouses and cormorants and rocks like turtle backs and whale skin rising out of the sea.

The man comes out the shop. 'Any problems with the car, sir?'

'No,' Dad says and hands the keys back. The man checks it over for bumps. We rub off specks of mud with our sleeves. I put my head next to Dad's. 'Tiny scratched the bonnet,' I whisper.

'I know,' he whispers back.

The man answers his phone and doesn't look properly.

He ticks the form and we walk off. Fast.

Down the hill to the white and red ferry that's waiting on the quay.

A woman with blond hair and wolf tattoos pulls the ropes and lowers the walkway down.

CLANG.

We walk over and on to the ship and strap the cases into the case place next to the motorbikes and climb up the stairs. Clank clank clank. We come out on the lounge deck and walk past maps of sea currents and people spreading out over seats with blankets and books.

Floyd and the shadow man are nowhere.

It feels wrong.

We go all the way to the back and I look out the window and see the flag fluttering off the end of the boat.

I look at everyone's faces.

Everyone might be *them*. They could be here and I wouldn't know.

I look for pieces of me. The colour of my hair. My nose. My freckles. My eyes.

She could have come early to check me out.

The air smells of coffee and heaters. I feel sick, like I can't breathe.

Dad looks at me. 'Do you wanna go outside?' he says.

I nod.

We push open the heavy metal doors and go out on to the back deck. Dad gets some cushions for the wet seats but me and Lloyd hold on to the rail and lean over.

Other families come out and pull the drawstrings on their hoods so their face is a tiny bumhole in the middle of their coats.

'It's too late,' Lloyd says and walks off to the end of the boat.

Two people come by with a chihuahua and walk round the corner. The chihuahua nearly blows over the edge with the wind blast. It's handy it's on a lead.

Dad leans over the edge and puts an arm round my shoulder. 'Not long now,' he says.

We pull away from the land.

Away
    Away
        Away.

We   pull   closer   into   the   unknown.
        Closer
    Closer
Closer.

We move forwards. We don't go back.

Her

Clonk.

Everyone jerks.

The boat bangs into the harbour tyres. Our heads bounce back.

'We're here,' Dad says.

The guard lowers the walkway. It clanks on the harbour and we untie the cases and rumble them over and on to the dock. It's concrete, sticking out from a bay. White sand, white sky, white light. Dad clutches his trumpet. We're the only people who get off.

The guard nods and hauls the walkway up again and the boat pulls away to the next island.

We are alone.

I look out at the emptiness. Hills and tracks lead off from the quay. There're no hotels or shops or anything. The mountains rise around us in layers with haze in between. We are *in* the Norway brochure. In the middle of nowhere. I look up at the sky. Dark clouds are squeezing in.

We look at each other.

Dad puts his hands on his hips. 'What now?'

'Someone's coming to meet us,' I say.

'Who?'

'Them.' I point. Over the hill comes a buzz and a man on a moped in a leather jacket. Dust clouds up behind him. He skids round us, flicks down the kickstand and gets off. When the dust drops, for a minute I think it might be *him*. I see he has hands the size of dinner plates, and earrings. It isn't.

He pulls his eye goggles on to his head. 'Which one of you is Elvis?' he says.

'He is.' They point at me.

The man sings 'Love Me Tender'.

Love me tender
Love me true
All my dreams fulfilled . . .

He stops.

'Kirsten sent me,' he says.

'Who?'

'You will see.' He slaps the wooden crate, stuck to the front of the moped. 'Put your cases on here.'

We put the cases on. 'See you,' he says and drives off.

He looks back over his shoulder. 'Too slow,' he yells. 'If you want to see where we are going you will need to be faster.'

We look at each other. The moped buzzes away. 'I think we should run,' I say.

And we run.

Lloyd runs like a spider on its back legs, arms waving free.

Dad runs like he's trying to look like someone that runs, knees up, arms pumping.

I run. I don't know how I run. Because I am me. And insides look different to outsides.

My arms and legs are moving disconnected from my brain. Everything is blurry and bouncy. Gravel gets in my shoes.

Two magpies stare at us from a tree with its branches chopped off.

I think,

This is weird.

> *This is weird.*

And we run into the weirdness. Over the white gravel, kicking up dust, under the sky with dark clouds and into stumpy trees.

The bike stops at a white wooden house. We stop too. My lungs go up and down. I think my face is purple. Dad's is.

The man gets off the moped and takes our cases out of the box. BANG. They hit the ground. Lloyd goes to check his apples for bruising.

'Where are you from?' the man says.

'The north of England,' I say.

'You mean Scotland,' he says.

'No.'

He shrugs and his earrings jingle. He gets on the bike.

'Who are you?' I say.

'You don't need to know,' he says and zooms off. He waves backwards and his ponytail bounces over the bumps.

I look at the house. It's got red window frames and balconies that pop out like ideas from a brain, and chains in the corners that hold the sides to the ground. Out the front there're two smaller cabins and animal sheds dotted about in a field. A white goat stands on the grass house roof staring at us and goes back to eating it. Three chickens walk by.

Five chairs sit under an awning.

Empty.

Out of the door comes a woman with long straight hair in a white shirt.

Her eyes are green. Her hair blows in the wind.

I don't know what to say. I feel hot and strange.

I think of all my visions. A mother, my mother?

I can't speak. No one else does either.

I don't hug her.

I don't move.

I just stand.

I thought I'd be angry.

I thought I'd be happy.

Actually, I just feel really weird.

'Elvis.' She looks at me. 'So you are Elvis.'

I nod.

And I think it's odd that she hasn't touched me

at

all

or even stroked my hair.

And I think of all the ways I thought this would go and I didn't expect to be this close.

And feel this much

d   i   s   t   a   n   c   e.

Going Backwards

We freeze-frame.

Both gripping our elbows.

Her eyes looking all over my face.

Her hair dancing. She tucks it behind an ear.

We've got the same colour hair. The same colour eyes. But I take a step back.

I think of Jean and Steinar: *Your body tells you things. The world is stronger than we know.*

Something in my stomach pulls.

I shake my head. The clouds block out the sun.

I don't know how I know it but I do. I know it from my guts to my lungs.

'It's not you.' I look her in the eyes. 'You aren't her.'

It isn't. She isn't. I know it.

She shakes her head.

I don't think her eyes even blink.

'No.' She nods. 'I am sorry.' She tilts her head. It's

hard to know if she means it. Her face is blank. 'The truth finds everyone.' She looks at me.

She turns and looks at Lloyd. 'The truth finds everyone in the end.'

Falling

My knees go weak. Dad puts an arm round my shoulders and pulls me in. His soft sweatshirt smells of home.

He sticks a hand out. 'I'm George,' he says.

The woman stares at him. 'You are Elvis's father.'

'Well yes,' Dad says, 'and no.' He rubs the back of his neck.

'You're his father,' she says. Her voice is sure and strong. She walks over to the table.

A blast of wind whips us all. The woman grabs her hair over one shoulder and looks behind.

Someone else comes out of the house. A girl. Brown hair, curly. Jeans and a big grey sweatshirt. She carries a tray of drinks and glasses.

'This is Lene,' Kirsten says and Lloyd falls over into a chair. 'Won't you please sit down.'

Waiting

Lene puts the glasses out on the table. Lloyd hunches. The chair holds him in tight like a pencil. He looks trapped.

And scared.

Of what?

Kirsten stares at him.

Lloyd puts his hands over his face like he doesn't want to be seen.

Me and Dad share a bench at the far end.

Lene pours out the drinks that nobody touches.

'Your parents were here. But not any more. I am sorry.' Kirsten looks at me. 'This is the way we speak on the islands. Truth is more important than evasion.'

It's good to just hear the truth.

'Is he here?' Lloyd says. 'Did he get here first?'

'I don't know what you are talking about,' she says and looks at me.

I look at her face. Her eyes are strong and green. 'Who are you?'

She takes a bottle out of a cupboard built into the grass and pours out three glasses.

The strength of it blows over and hits me like a slap.

'I am Kirsten,' she says. 'Welcome to your birthplace, Elvis. I've been waiting a very long time to see you.'

In

Lene picks up a black cat and swings it over her shoulder. Its paws hang down her back.

Two kittens run out of the doorway and into the hill cupboard.

Lloyd stares at Lene.

Kirsten stares at Lloyd.

I'm full of questions but nothing comes out.

'Come.' Kirsten drinks her drink and rubs her hands on her sides. 'You must be hungry . . .'

I'm not.

The idea of eating makes me feel sick.

She turns round, goes into the house.

Lene looks at the drinks and back at Kirsten and goes in too.

The door's like a mouth sucking up everyone.

'You OK?' Dad squeezes my shoulder. Rain starts to drip on our heads.

'I dunno.' I don't. But I stand up. 'I wanna go in.'

Dad picks up his drink and downs it in one. He slaps his chest and coughs.

Lloyd doesn't say anything and starts biting his fingers. He looks like a dog that just opened the bin all over the kitchen floor.

His head hangs, his eyes are low.

Why?

'Floyd isn't here,' I say. 'He didn't get here first, Lloyd.'

'I know,' he says. 'I know.'

I take his hand. I take Dad's. And we walk into the house.

The three of us.

The new meeting the past.

I walk back in to where I left off.

Hurry

We go through a red doorframe into the dark.

I shut my eyes and blink to get used to it. The room is wide with wooden floors and a set of stairs at the back. It's full of big windows with no curtains and chairs with bright cushions and cats.

They raise their heads and blink at us and go back to sleep.

Lene sits on the sofa doing something on an iPad. It looks weird seeing one out here.

The table's laid out with planks of wood.

With cheese.

And bread.

And jam on.

'You have a lot to think about right now,' Kirsten says. 'It's not a good time for talking. We will only say unimportant things that we don't really mean.' She puts a record on the deck on the shelf. The needle hisses on the vinyl and she cranks the volume up.

Music blasts out. The sounds push against our skin and try to come into us.

I walk over to the record and take the needle off.

'I want to know the truth.'

'What is your hurry?' Kirsten rubs her elbow.

'There is danger.' Lloyd looks at the floor. 'For everyone.'

She flips her head to Lloyd. 'Really, why?' Her voice is like ice.

'Lloyd's brother,' I say. 'Floyd.'

Kirsten prickles. She looks at Lloyd. 'Floyd?' Lloyd looks at the floor.

'This isn't about him. It's about me.' I grip the empty compass space in my pocket. 'I want to know 'cos it's my life and I've been waiting twelve years to know it. That isn't a hurry. It's just how it is.'

I look out the window. The sky is grey and coming fast like shadows. Everything is closing in like an argument. The front door blows open and three cats run in with their ears down and two kittens hide in some shoes. The wind is pushing its arms through the door hole and grabbing things and moving them around. Paper, packets, our hair.

'It is time,' Kirsten says. Rains starts throwing

itself against the windows like a car wash. I didn't know storms hit this fast, this hard. 'To the awning!' she yells.

'What?'

'RUN!'

We all run outside.

White froth from the sea spits over the grass and the rocks. The island shrinks and is more blue than green. We cling on to the poles and try to unhook the awning. We take a corner each and Lloyd hops about in the middle. The rain slaps our faces and the canvas jolts up and my arm nearly snaps off. I hold on and wrap myself around the post.

We cling on to the poles.

We cling on to each other.

The awning is unhooked and blasts away into a tree like a ghost on the run. Lloyd shouts, 'Whooo,' and we chase after it, grab it and run back to the house with it stuffed under our arms.

Kirsten shoulders the door shut. It's a weird quiet. Our ears are full of whistling, like seashells. The wind sulks and kicks the door in again and throws a stick at the window.

We push it back and Kirsten slides the bolt over.

'Everyone deserves truth.' She nods and walks back over to the table. 'Please sit.'

She looks at Lloyd. Then Dad. Then me.

We sit round the table and wipe the water off our faces.

Lene goes back to the iPad.

Dad rubs his moustache.

Lloyd scrapes his chair back. 'I can't take this. I can't take it,' he says and runs upstairs like there's something she's gonna say he's terrified of.

Kirsten doesn't even blink. She picks up a white cat snaking round her ankles. 'This is what you want?'

I nod.

Why wouldn't I?

I've been waiting all my life.

'OK.' She nods and brings the cat up by her chin. 'Let's begin.'

The Truth and Not the Truth

The house does its best to hold us while the walls take on the storm outside. Tins and pans rattle in the kitchen. I think the wind might smash in through the windows but it doesn't. 'This house used to be a farm.' Kirsten puts the cat down and spreads out her arms. 'A long time ago. Twelve years ago.'

'Exactly?'

'Exactly.'

Like me. I swallow. A mug falls off the shelf. No one moves.

'I took on woofers. Workers on organic farms. People came from all over the world. We had animals, vegetables, everything . . .'

'My parents worked here?'

'Yes.' She nods. 'We were great friends. But they had some problems.'

'Like what?'

247

'Money, and drugs.' She sighs. 'They were unpredictable.'

'Oh.' I scratch my fingernail under the table.

'Your mother became pregnant.'

'On drugs?'

'No. She came off everything for that. I helped her through.' She opens her hands. 'Life is complicated.' She looks out. 'You were born under this table. You were very pink. And loud.' She smiles. 'Your mother was very tired so I held you in a towel and sang until you fell asleep. Then after two weeks you were gone.'

I think how I record sounds to fill the silence.

So I've always got something to block it out with.

Maybe that's why I started.

'Your mother is ...' She looks down at her fingers ... 'Your parents stole money from me and left for England.' She stands up, wraps her arms round her waist. 'That's all I know,' she says and walks out.

Forget It

The wind blasts through the open door and into our faces like a kid that's just won and wants to rub it in.

I try to push it away.

It laughs past my fingers.

The truth sits in my stomach like a worm I can't spit out.

I get up.

'Elvis.' Dad tries to catch me.

I shake my head and twist away. 'I wanna go out.'

'In that?' A piece of tree bounces off the window. Dad's eyes bunch together.

I go for the door. 'Yeah.'

He tries to catch my arm. I pull it away and go.

Out into the full force of the storm. A jackdaw gets chucked about and thrown back into its nest in the wall with a stick that's way too big to fit in. It hangs on to the stick.

I see the shadow of Kirsten standing, arms folded, hair flying.

I turn away, down the path kicking up rocks. My eyes are rain-sting blind slits. Sand is drilling into my skin and under my sleeves. Purple light comes at me from all sides, poking and prodding its way under my jumper and down my socks.

I think about the *Aftenposten*.

We share sixty per cent of our DNA with tomatoes and we are nothing like tomatoes.

I think about Jean and Steinar.

You are not all the time guessing.

I think about Bjorn.

His chainsaw badger bounces in my head.

I get down to the water and curl up into the grass.

And think about my life.

How I always felt like a loose piece of puzzle rattling in a box and all the other bits had fallen out, And I didn't know what the picture was on the front. Or what kind of shape I was meant to make. I just wanted to build some edges to give me something to hold on to. So I could fill in the gaps.

Now I've got edges.

And I just want to tear them all to pieces.

Reaching Out

Someone touches me on the shoulder.

I don't look up.

'I'm not going back, Dad.'

'I'm not your dad.'

I look round. It's Lene. Embarrassing.

I hold my hands up sideways like cheek wipers.

'My eyes hurt,' I yell.

'Yes.'

'And my ears.'

'Yes.' she says.

'I hate this stupid storm,' I scream and the storm carries on and takes no notice.

My trousers are soaking.

A massive bird makes a weird noise and swoops over us. It cocks its head sideways checking us out.

'White-tailed eagle.' Lene points. 'He lost his mate last winter.

The eagle bounces off. Whipped on the wind.

I wonder how much she heard before. She was on the iPad. Maybe she wasn't listening.

'My dad's dead, actually,' she shouts and squats down in the grass. 'If it helps.'

OK, so maybe she heard everything.

I don't know what to say to that. We turn away from a sand blast. 'Sorry,' I say. It's weird not being the one with the problem.

'He died when I was a baby.' She ducks a twig. 'I never met him.'

We watch a jellyfish blub up on to the sand, spat out of the waves.

'Your mum seems nice,'

'Your dads seem nice,'

we say together.

Lene half smiles.

'They're not my dads,'

'That's not my mum,'

we say in sync.

'She's my aunt.' She pulls her hair into her fist. 'I come here every summer.'

'Dad's my dad. Lloyd's his best friend,' I say. 'Actually he's more like a family pet we look after.'

She smiles. And out at sea one patch of sky turns

white in the middle of the purple. 'The weather's like this here,' she says. 'It does what it wants. In the winter the winds can get up to seventy miles an hour.'

'Is that why you chain the house down?' I imagine flying houses.

'Yeah.' She nods. 'Kirsten left her guitar on the top of that one last year and it ended up on the next island.' She points.

I wonder what kind of music the wind made when it flew. Does wind play guitar?

'In winter there's only three to four hours of sun.' She wipes the drips off her nose. 'And the snow is higher than your head.'

I don't think I could live like that.

We hunch up and watch the storm.

It howls in our faces.

And flattens our hair.

Neither of us moves.

Or says anything.

And it should feel weird.

But it doesn't.

It feels nice.

Kind of.

I take my phone out.

'What are you doing?'

'Recording.' I yell. 'I like sounds.'

She nods at the phone. I record:

stormy thoughtful

(a massive rip-it-up storm, hiss and crackle).

'I sing,' she says.

'Cool.' It takes three stabs to switch my phone off as my fingers are numb. I put it back in my pocket. 'I make videos.' I think about the comments string. 'Well I used to. People are mean.'

'People are always mean.' She stands up. 'You should do it anyway.' The water rolls off her waterproofs. She stretches her arms up and screams. 'Sometimes it is a good thing to do.' She grins.

I look around. There's no one to see us. There's no one here for miles. Who's gonna hear it anyway? So I stand up and scream too. It's like all the stuff that's bad comes out from inside for a while. And it feels good.

I watch my anger rolling round the mountains.

We scream some more.

And I realise that I'm smiling. Even though my hands are blue.

Lene wrings the water out of her hair.

A woman walks past, bent double and acting like nothing is happening.

'Who's that?'

'Mrs Halvardson,' Lene waves.

'*Hei hei!*' Mrs Halvardson holds her hood with one hand. 'Misty needs walking.' Her dog is jumping about, its tongue lolling. Its eyes big and bright. Misty's neck and front legs float off his lead.

'We should go in,' Lene says and starts walking back to the house.

'Will you sneak me upstairs?'

I don't wanna see Kirsten right now. It's so embarrassing. She quit her farm 'cos of me.

'I don't need to sneak you,' Lene looks over her shoulder. 'That's where you're staying. I made your beds up this afternoon.' She keeps walking. 'Coming or what?'

A leaf slaps me on the cheek. I pull it off and follow.

Home

Inside there's no sign of Kirsten. Lene leads the way through the house. We drip up one floor with a wooden landing and rooms leading off, and she shows me the bathroom with a hamster in the bath. 'He's called Sumo,' she says. 'He lives there for freedom, to escape a cage.' She passes me a dressing gown and waits outside. Sumo scuttles through a toilet tube with a mouth full of sunflower seeds.

I peel off my clothes which are stuck like Pritt Stick and run my hands under the hot tap till they turn pink.

I wonder why Kirsten walked out?

I wonder what she knew about my mother but didn't say?

Why?

I wonder why Floyd and his shadow aren't here?

The dressing gown hangs down to my ankles. Lene doesn't laugh.

'Did anyone strange come to the island last night?'

'Like who?'

'Two men.'

'No.' Lene takes off her waterproofs and everything is dry underneath. 'Maybe.' She dumps her trousers in the sink. 'If they came on their own boat. I can only see the ferry from here.'

We walk through the house and up into an attic with windows all down one side. The floor is bright blue with strawberry wallpaper and two beds, one down by the windows, one in the corner, with fairy lights and Dad on. When he sees me he smiles.

'You can shut the panel if you want to be alone.' Lene points at a wooden panel which hinges from the floor. She shows us how it shuts and blocks off the stairs. 'This is Rufus.' She hands me a black kitten. 'This is Garfield.' She hands Dad a white one and goes off downstairs.

'Bye,' I yell after her.

'See yer,' she yells back.

The kittens wriggle in our hands.

I sit next to Dad.

Rufus rolls on his back and bops the air.

Garfield climbs up Dad's chest and sniffs his armpit. 'I'm sorry it didn't work out how you wanted.' He sighs. The window bounces open and lets the storm in.

I think about my parent dreams.

What did I expect.

Loving arms and a sweet sad story of how much I was missed and how they've spent their whole life searching for me?

Yes actually.

A part of my insides squeezes.

Yeah that is what I wanted.

I feel really stupid.

At least now I know the truth.

Do I?

I put my hands under the kittens' fur so the purring goes right through me.

Dad puts an arm round my shoulder. 'You OK?'

'No,' I say and laugh. It's unexpected. It just bubbles right out of me. 'Where's Lloyd?'

'Staying in one of the cabins.' Dad points out the window.

'Why'd he run out, Dad? What does he know we don't?'

'You know Lloyd. Everything about him is a mystery.' Dad stares out at the island. 'Look at it.

It's the wildest most beautiful place I've ever seen in my life,' he says and we watch the curtains dance. 'You want to stay for a while?' He tickles Rufus under the chin. 'Kirsten wants to show you around.'

'She doesn't hate me?'

'Why would she hate you?'

'I messed up her life.'

'You didn't,' he says and turns my head. 'It wasn't anything to do with you. You didn't do anything wrong. Kirsten said she's happy you're back.'

'When was that?'

'When she came back in.'

'What else did she say?'

'Nothing.' Dad's voice sounds squeaky.

'Stuff about me?'

'Get in bed before you go blue –' he looks away – 'and I'll put the kettle on.'

'Too late, I already went blue.' I follow his eyes, but he doesn't look at me. 'And why's Floyd disappeared?'

'Beats me, Sherlock,' he says. 'And good riddance.'

'Don't you care?'

He clicks the kettle on and rubs his eyes. 'Go to

sleep, Miss Marple,' he says. 'Before I have to give you a tranquilliser dart.'

He mimes giving me one in my arm and we laugh and get into bed and I lie there drinking raspberry tea which I think will taste like Ribena but doesn't, and eating biscuits which look like digestives but aren't.

And I think how it should all feel like I know everything now.

Like it's all ended.

But I don't.

Voices

In the night I wake up.

The storm's gone flat. The wind is nowhere.

Light comes through the window.

The alarm clock flashes 12.13.

I twitch the curtain and look at the midnight sun.

And Lloyd.

And Kirsten.

'I didn't know she was here,' he says.

'Why would I tell you?' Kirsten has her arms folded. 'You haven't told Elvis the truth? If you don't tell the truth, how can you expect to receive it?'

'You don't know what he's like.' Lloyd paces around. 'He's dangerous. I thought he was coming for us. He isn't. He can't be.' He points at the sea. 'He's coming for her.'

'You're his family, Lloyd. You should have told him.'

Lloyd looks up.

Right at me.

I jump and shut the curtain.

They go quiet.

Did he see me?

Does it matter?

If they're talking about me I've got a right to know it.

A door creaks and bangs.

I jump up and run downstairs, through one flight and two.

You're his family, Lloyd.

Like how? Metaphorically like Dad? I guess so.

He's coming. Floyd? *For her.* Who?

The only her is Lene?

I run through the lounge and fling open the door.

But they have disappeared like ghosts.

You?

I get back into bed and have the mirror dream again.

The one from Steinar's.

I'm in that room.

It's freaky.

And cold.

And the window's open.

The mirror's there standing in the middle.

And this time it isn't one hand, it's two coming out. Fast and strong.

Searching, searching and reaching. I run back.

My head hits the wall.

I look in the mirror.

This time I can see the face.

But it isn't my reflection.

It isn't me.

It's . . .

Aghh

I wake up covered in sweat.

Lene is standing on the stairs' hatch staring at me.

'Aghh,' I yell.

Dad rolls and grunts but doesn't wake up.

'What are you doing?'

'I don't know,' she says and rubs her eyes. 'You were yelling.'

We stare at each other.

'I need to find Lloyd.' I get out of bed in the dressing gown. 'Him and Kirsten were arguing last night.'

'About what?'

We go through the hatch, down both sets of stairs.

'I dunno. I need to ask him. What cabin's he in?'

'That one.' She opens the door and points. 'I think.'

We kick our shoes on and go out into the grass. The mountains fold their arms and stare at us. The dew soaks my shoes.

I open the cabin door.

Lloyd's case is there. His apples are there. His books are there.

But Lloyd isn't.

'Maybe he just went for a walk.' Lene shrugs.

'I don't think so.' Something feels wrong.

We run back into the house.

I follow Lene through the beady curtain and into the kitchen. It is very long and thin with shelves full of pots and pans and tins and jars and a window that looks out over the rocks. The view's like layers, like those sand pots with different colours in stripes. Rock, grass, sky. There are no cupboard doors.

Kirsten stands looking out the window. The blue gas on the stove bubbles under a kettle.

'Lloyd's gone!'

'People are free to go as they choose,' she says.

The kettle starts to whistle and scream. Kirsten switches it off.

'We need to find him.' I look at Lene. 'Maybe Floyd took him. Maybe he's been kidnapped.'

'He hasn't.' Kirsten scoops coffee into a glass pot.

'How do you know?'

She pours water in. The smell coils round us. 'I told him to go. Lorenzo took him in his boat.'

'The guy on the motorbike.' Lene gets a biscuit out of a jar.

Kirsten nods.

'Why?'

She looks at Lene. She looks at me. Her eyes go misty. 'It should never have been left this long,' she says and goes outside and sits on a bench.

Lene wipes crumbs on her sleeve. 'Has he got a phone?'

'Lloyd?'

'Yeah. Find him on that. Use Find a Friend,' she says. 'It's easy.'

Dad comes down and wipes his eyes. 'What's up?'

'Lloyd's missing.' I point at the door. 'Ask Kirsten. She sent him away.'

The wheel spins round on the phone.

Connecting

Connecting

    Connected.

We see him.

Nowhere near here.

The blue flashing dot of Lloyd is way off.

Way out over the sea on an island.

'He's on Traena.' Lene wrinkles her face. 'There's a music festival there.'

'How do you know?'

'That's where my mum is. She goes every year.'

'You don't go?'

'You don't know my mum.' She shoves another biscuit in her mouth. 'You could ring him,' she says.

I click on Lloyd.

It rings.

And rings.

And rings.

He doesn't pick up. 'He won't answer.'

'He's got his own life.' Dad pours out a coffee.

I pick up a kitten. It purrs in my neck. 'Can you ring your mum?' If you ring her, maybe she can find him. Maybe she can check he's OK?'

Lene hesitates. She breathes out.

'Elvis.' Dad looks at me. 'You don't have to, Lene. Lloyd's an adult. He can take care of himself.'

'With Floyd?' I look at Dad. 'Lloyd's never been able to handle Floyd. He's bullied him his whole life.'

'It's OK.' Lene clicks her phone. 'I'm doing it.'

It doesn't say Mum, it says *Nina*.

Weird.

She holds it to her ear.

BEEEEP

BEEEEP

BEEEEP.

It answers.

'Hey, Mum.'

'Lene?'

I can hear her voice out the other side of the phone.

'I need you to find someone ... He's a friend. Kind of ... It's a man. Have you seen a man ...'

'A man?'

'Yeah.'

'The man?'

'Lloyd?'

'How do you know about Floyd? What do you know?'

'Nothing ...'

'I don't know what to do, Lene. We could use some money couldn't we?'

'What are you on about?'

'I have to go.'

The line goes dead.

BEEEEEEEEEEEEEEEEEEEEP.

It's Time

Lene tries to ring back.

But can't.

'She's switched her phone off.' She bangs it on the table.

I stare at her. 'Your mum knows Floyd?'

'No. I dunno. I don't think so. Who's Floyd?'

'Lloyd's brother. He's trying to kill us.'

'He hasn't tried to kill us.' Dad hovers behind us.

'Why are you sticking up for him?' I turn round.

'I'm not!' Dad puts his hands up.

'How come you and your mum speak in English?'

'My dad was English, so she makes me keep it up. She lived there for a while.' Lene kicks her foot into a cupboard.

'Why would Floyd offer your mum money?'

'I have no idea. Is he rich?'

'Yeah, but . . .' I rub my head.

'What?'

'He likes to keep it for himself.'

'Maybe Lloyd doesn't want to be found,' Dad says.

'Why? He had an argument with Kirsten last night. She said he was my family.'

Dad goes white. 'That could mean lots of things,' he says and rubs his neck.

I think of point six on how to know when people are lying.

Self grooming.

What does he know that I don't?

'And now she's sent him away.'

Lene pulls my sleeve. 'The goat needs milking,' she says and drags me outside.

We huddle round the back of the long red shed.

'You got a rucksack right?'

I nod.

'Pack it and meet me by the back door.'

'With what?'

'Clothes, waterproofs, spare stuff,' she says. 'We can go in my boat.'

I wipe a cobweb off my hair. 'You've got a boat?'

'Everyone has boats. We learn it when we're like five.'

I keep staring.

'I'm sea-scout sailing champion,' she says. 'Under fourteen category. Trust me or what?'

'OK.' I nod.

The goat eats the bottom of my jumper.

'This is Nancy,' Lene says. 'She really does need milking.'

Away

Lene leads Nancy along by the collar and her bell clangs.

We shuffle into a red shed.

She gets out a wooden stool and sits on it. 'Can you get some dandelions?'

'Why?'

'They're her favourite.'

I go outside and stuff my pockets full.

When I get back I hear the rhythm of the milk squirting against the side of a bucket. I hold a dandelion near Nancy and she swipes it out of my hand.

I rub her horn bumps. She seems to like it. She bites my pocket for more dandelions.

'If Floyd tried to kill you, offering Mum money can't be good. We need to find her.'

'Money to do what?' I say.

'Exactly,' she says.

'I hate secrets.'

'I know what it's like. Not to know stuff. I know how it feels to be stopped.' Lene says. She doesn't stop squirting. 'My mum blames herself for my dad dying. So she never talks about it.'

'What happened?'

'They had a row, then he left and drove into a tree.' She wipes her hair out of her face with the back of her hand. 'Sometimes she just feels like a brick wall.'

I think of the mirror dream, reaching in like there's secrets stuck behind it. 'I know what you mean.'

Nancy guzzles all the dandelions and Lene fills the bucket.

She pours the milk into a jug and then filters it into glass bottles which she puts in a freezer.

We walk back into the house.

Dad's chainsawing logs out the front with Kirsten. I don't look at them.

We walk in and split into our own rooms.

When I come down Lene is already waiting out the back. I don't know how she can be that fast.

'Stay there,' she whispers. 'I'm going in for food.'

I watch through the crack of the open door as

Lene slips in like a cat and stashes stuff off the shelves into her bag. Biscuits, crisps, crackers, a tube of pink stuff out of the fridge and two bottles of water.

Kirsten comes in and Lene slides round the side of the fridge.

I flatten my back against the wall.

Kirsten gets a pack of biscuits and leaves.

Lene climbs on top of the flatbed freezer and pulls dried fish down from a hook in the ceiling. The hook goes through the eyehole. She winks at me. 'You like *tørfisk*?'

I haven't tried it but I'm guessing husky dried-out fish meat isn't gonna be my favourite.

I pull a dead-fish face.

She puts her finger on her lips and tries not to laugh.

'Let's go.' She climbs down, stuffs the fish in her bag and we turn away from the house, towards the sun.

Happy?

We walk down the path and fork right up a hill. The track zigzags up and up.

The sun makes the grass glow emerald-green. I feel like we're going up into the sky. Which spreads out turquoise. We reach the summit and look down at a small bay, a small beach and a jetty.

Oystercatchers waddle along. Pipping.

I like their beaks.

Lene points down at her boat bouncing, red, white and blue. 'Don't laugh at the name,' she says. 'It's bad luck to change it.'

'How do you even get a boat?' We walk along the ridge and drop down. I shield the sun out of my eyes.

'I got it for my birthday one summer. When I was eight,' she says. 'Off Kirsten. So I could sail myself over that summer, every summer.' She kicks a rock over the edge of the path. 'So I could sail over whenever I needed.'

'Do you need to?'

She keeps walking. 'Sometimes,' she says. 'Sometimes I need a break.'

'From what?'

'Does it matter?'

'Yeah.'

'You haven't met my mother,' she says.

I think of the voice on the phone. The way she hung up.

'This is my bay.'

'It's beautiful,' I say. It totally is.

I look at the boat bobbing in the glittery water. It's wooden with a small cabin, with the wheel and windscreen at the front and round windows on the sides.

We clank down the jetty. The water slaps the wood.

I read the side:

Den Glade Gullfisk

What does that mean?'

'The Happy Goldfish,' she says. 'I told you not to laugh.'

Sperm Whales Can Swallow Whole Boats

We do laugh though. We laugh all the way till I chuck my bag in the back of the boat and two hard blue eyes pop up and chuck it back on the jetty.

'Lene,' I yell, 'watch out!'

But Lene's picked up an oar out of the front and is holding it over her head. 'Get out of my boat!' she says and swings it at his face.

The shadow man ducks and sidesteps. She swings again. He grabs on to the end of the pole. I grab on to Lene. It's our strength against his. 'Your orders are not to leave this island,' he pulls us in. Our feet skid along the wood.

I think about the hotel. Don't defend. Attack. Attack!

I let go of the oar. The force of it snaps him backwards. Lene flies into the *Gullfisk*. She stands up and passes me another oar.

I bring it over my head and smack it down on to his. He falls over sideways, eyes shut.

'Pull the rope.' Lene points.

I pull the boat into the jetty and climb in. 'Did I kill him?'

Lene kicks his ankle. He groans. 'No,' she says. 'Take his legs.'

I grab his legs and she takes his arms and we drag him out of the boat on to the jetty.

'Who is he?' Lene squats next to his face.

'Floyd's detective,' I say and pull my compass out of his jacket.

I stuff it back into my pocket.

We roll him on to his front and pull his arms together and Lene goes into the boat and comes out with a piece of blue twine and a knife. 'Will it hold him?' I look at the mooring rope. It's loads thicker.

'I'm not cutting the mooring rope,' she says and looks at me like I just killed her hamster.

'What if he comes after us?'

'He won't if you tie it tight enough.' Lene slices the twine in two. We take half each and do his arms and legs. I tie as tight as I know how and roll him on to his side.

'In case he's sick,' I say. I know that much from PSHE first aid.

If he chokes on sick he dies. If he dies I'll go to prison, won't I?

Lene pulls the *Gullfisk* in to the jetty and we chuck our bags in the back. I jump in. She unties the rope and jumps in too.

'If he's touched anything in here I'll go back and kill him myself,' she says and checks over everything with her fingers.

'Won't they notice we're gone?' I step into the cabin.

'Who?'

'Dad and Kirsten.'

'Let them notice. They're keeping secrets from us, right?' She looks back at the jetty. 'Did they know he was here?'

'No!' I tap my elbow. Why would Kirsten send Lloyd away otherwise? 'I don't think so.' I look at the man. Not moving. 'On the way here Floyd shot at us. I thought he wanted to scare us away.'

'From what?' We pull life jackets over our heads and clip them on. She starts the engine. It smells of diesel.

The boat buzzes underneath us.

279

'I thought he wanted us to go home. Lloyd said he wanted us to give up. Now he's disappeared. It doesn't make sense.'

A light on the dashboard flashes and I think about pressing it. I don't. Brain-flick control.

'He hasn't disappeared.' Lene grits her teeth. 'He's with my mum.'

I tap the dashboard. 'Hmmn.'

We bob out to sea like a little petrol-driven cork. The waves are shallow and rolling. I try to roll with them and not to feel sick.

I wonder what he wants.

Why do people offer people money?

Blackmail?

People try to *get* money for that. Not *give* it.

'Maybe she knows something he doesn't want us to know. Maybe he's trying to pay her off?'

'Like what?'

I get Lene's bag off the floor. 'You hungry?'

She nods.

I'm starving.

Lene gets out a packet of crackers and squirts pink stuff all over. It looks like brains.

'You want to try some?'

280

I pull a face.

'Everyone makes it here. The kids chop out the tongues.'

I stick mine out and get out a big bag of crisps in the shape of lighthouses.

'Kirsten said something last night.' I eat a handful. 'She said Lloyd should have told me the truth.'

'About what?'

'She didn't say.' White water bubbles over the front of the boat. We bounce down.

'People are weird about my dad too,' Lene says. 'No one ever wants to talk about him. Sometimes people just don't like the past.'

'Do you know what he looked like?'

'We have one photo.' She pulls a locket out of her shirt and drops it back down. 'I like to carry him around.'

'I've got my dad's dad's dad's compass,' I say and pull it out of mine. 'Well, I have now.' It's good to have it back.

'At least you have a dad,' Lene says. 'You actually have two.'

We stand there crunching and looking out at the water squished up together like orange balloons

in a fish tank. I think about that. I have two dads.
It's true.

'What's that?' I say and point at rolling black humps
that bob up and down. Water squirts up as they rise.
I go out through the cabin and lean over the edge.
I see five black and white backs dipping and rolling.

Lene yells from the cabin, 'That's a pod of orcas.'

'Nice.'

She looks over her shoulder. 'If they come this
way, they could roll us over, or smash the boat.'

I look down and feel the power in their bodies.

PSHHHHH

PSHHHHH.

I see one eye. It turns away.

I watch them drift off into the blue.

'They're going,' I say and wobble-walk back into
the cabin.

'Sperm whales can swallow whole boats.' She
switches on the radio. 'Not that they want to – just
that their mouths are so big they can.'

I look at the black backs dipping away.

'Why are there so many?'

'Orcas always swim in pods,' Lene says. 'They
always stick with their families.'

Messed Up

'Human families are messed up.' I tip out the last of the crisps.

'True.' Lene stares out the windscreen.

I look out at the water.

You're his family.

What did Kirsten mean?

You have two dads.

It's true. Isn't it?

Something clicks in my head. Something dark and weird.

And scary.

I try to push the idea out.

But it won't go.

What if she wasn't being metaphorical?

What if she actually really meant it?

I play back over our lives like a film. In flashbacks.

When we got here Kirsten acted weird with Lloyd.

The truth finds everyone, she said. *The truth finds everyone in the end.*

Why is Lloyd always around?

Why did he pay for the trip in the first place?

I go further back. Right to the beginning.

I'm paying, Lloyd said. *It's the least I can do.*

He shook my Babygro. He knew the note was meant to be in it. How?

He'd only know it if he put it there.

He'd only put it there if he knew it himself.

He'd only put it there if it was him.

It was him who left me.

The Ks match.

Because he wrote it.

The truth hits me in the face.

I look at Lene. 'What if Lloyd's my dad?' I say.

She spits out a crisp. 'That's ridiculous.'

'Is it?' I read about people whose sisters turned out to be their mums because they couldn't cope. So their grandma brought them up. Together. Maybe Lloyd couldn't cope?'

I think about

'Sometimes Lloyd can't cope with being Lloyd. That's why he comes round ours.'

We pull into an island that looks like a giant dragon's tooth coming up out of the water. Like something out of *Jurassic World*. 'I don't think it's ridiculous,' I say. Eagles glide in on the thermals. 'I think it makes everything make sense.'

Say It

'Right,' Lene says. 'So why is he offering Mum money?'

'Maybe she knows, maybe he's paying her not to say?'

'My mum knows Lloyd?'

'Maybe.'

'How?'

'How would I know?'

'Don't take it out on me.' She switches off the radio.

'I'm not.'

Other boats go by. They fly flags and wave and honk and whoop. Their music drifts in and out.

I hear the music booming from the main stage. I look up. There's lights even though it's light. You can see the colours.

Pink.

Purple.

Green.

We pull into the harbour. The jetties are thick with boats. Masts and decks and sails and engines. Hundreds of them.

We have to steer and squeeze in tight.

Lene hops out. I pass the rope over and she squats and ties us to the jetty.

People are having boat parties. Smoke drifts over. Girls are jumping in and climbing out of the water and the air is full of screaming and singing.

The bass from the main stage digs into my ribs. It's nice.

We look at the sea of people and scramble out of the lifejackets.

I look up Lloyd on my phone. The blue dot flashes. I take Lene's hand. 'This way.' I pull her. She lets go. 'I can take myself,' she says and we run through people with no hair and full body tattoos and dancers and people kissing and cans of lager and yoga headstands. In and out of smells and bodies and down through the rocks, over the grass and straight into Lloyd. He runs at us and grabs Lene by both arms. 'Thank goodness you're here.' He shakes her. 'You need to tell her. She won't believe me. Tell your mother not to sign.'

'Ow. Get off.' Lene pulls away.

I take Lloyd's arm. He swings round. Confused.

I look right into his face. This person I've known all my life.

'Cept maybe I haven't. Maybe I thought I did. Maybe it's all just been a lie.

Say it, I think.

Just say it.

'Lloyd,' I say. 'Are you my dad?'

He looks at me. His face falls.

'No, Elvis,' he says and the world slows right down. 'I am your uncle.'

Go

Uncle?

Uncle means brother. Brother of father. Who is Lloyd's brother?

Floyd.

It's Floyd.

Floyd?

Floyd is my dad?

'NO!' I yell. 'No!'

I pull my energy into my bones and run. I run past skin and rocks and grass and fires and smoke. I run through screams and laughter and faces and darkness. I don't ever want to stop.

He didn't want me to meet my mother 'cos she'd tell me.

He doesn't want me to meet her 'cos he doesn't want me to know.

I jump over stretched-out legs and stomachs and down to the jetty.

I feel the compass in my pocket.

My grandad's grandad's blood.

It's in me through Dad.

I'm more him than anyone.

I'm more Lucas than Partington.

I bang into a body on the jetty. Head down. I look up. 'Dad?'

Kirsten is tying a boat to the dock.

'Elvis?' Dad puts a hand to my chest like a barrier.

I dodge it. 'Leave me alone.'

I jump into Lene's boat and unwind the rope.

Dad and Kirsten run. Dad grabs the rope on the dock. I pull it. 'Let me go.' I pull hard. He slips. I fall back and my head hits the wood. Dad loses his balance.

He doesn't fall back. He falls down. Down over the edge. I hear the splash.

I do what Lene did. I switch the engine on and go. I can't stop.

I'm drifting away.

Wipe Out

I don't know what I'm doing.

I scrape along the bow of a white yacht. Someone yells.

I look back for Dad and see his head bobbing, his hand reaching for the jetty, a crowd gathering round.

The *Gullfish* moves on, out into the waves. Into the middle of nowhere.

I feel tiny.

And scared.

The water rolls the boat, playing with it like it knows I don't know what I'm doing.

My stomach pulses.

What am I? A past Floyd doesn't want to own up to? That'd destroy him.

I lean over the side and am sick.

I sick up every part of me that might belong to him and switch the engine off.

The boat eddies and spins.

I sink down into the bottom and curl up.
I am a ball, curled up inside itself.
No one can reach me.
'Cos I'm a phone with a black screen.
And zero battery.
And everything wiped off from the inside.

Sucker Punch

I don't know how long I stay like that.

I hear a

             PSHHHHH

and a

                       PSHHHHH.

The boat creaks.

        click

            whirr

        click.

It rises on one side.

I look up and see a mist creeping over. White swirls pushing in.

I look over the edge and see a black nose.

White back.

Black fin.

One, two . . . three of them.

Orcas.

Killer whales.

Pure meat and muscle.

293

A head bobs up. A back.

They get closer.

One noses the boat.

It creaks.

This is it, I think.

I'm gonna die. I'm gonna die in the sea.

Tears pour down my face.

'Do it,' I say, shaking. 'If you're gonna do it. Just do it.'

But they don't do anything.

One looks me right in the eye. We stare at each other like it's reading my brain.

It dives.

I hear the buzz of an engine. I can't see anything. The mist is too strong.

When I look back I see the whales' heads and bodies rolling away.

Slinking off into the sea.

And a white yacht pings out of the mist. It's coming this way.

Big.

Posh.

High out of the water.

And I think it can only be one person.

He knows I know.

It's Floyd.

It's Floyd coming for me.

If he comes here I'll punch him.

It he tries to touch me I'll sock him in the face.

All this time Floyd just didn't want me to find out.

I'm an embarrassment am I?

A dark bit of MP Floyd Partington's life that he doesn't want to admit to.

That'll ruin his career.

His shiny family-friendly face.

The engine stops.

It drifts alongside.

A face hangs over.

It isn't Floyd. It's Lloyd.

'I've got nothing to say to you.' I turn my back on him and drop on to the floor.

The boat rocks.

'Your father isn't Floyd,' Lloyd says. 'He isn't Floyd, Elvis.'

Like how.

I don't turn round.

'It's my other brother Boyd,' he says. 'It's Boydy.'

What Happened

'Who's he?' I turn round.

Lloyd drops his head.

'He died, Elvis. He died just after you were born.'

Dead?

I go cold and am suddenly sick again. Over the side of the boat.

'My little brother.' Lloyd hangs his head. 'I wish you could have met him.' He puts his hands over his ears. I splash salty water over my face. It sets tight.

Lloyd bobs closer. 'I would come aboard –' he waves his hands in front of the controls – 'but this is Floyd's boat. I nicked it. I have actually no idea what I'm doing.' He laughs. 'Boyd would have been proud. I miss him.'

'Your own brother.' I wipe my mouth with my sleeve. 'And you never said. Twelve years and you never said.'

Lloyd hangs his head. 'My family never speaks of him. I did what I thought was best. I gave you

George. He is the best man I know.' He frowns. 'They came to my house,' he says. 'From Norway. They had nowhere to go.'

'My parents?'

He nods. 'Boyd wanted to see Father. He hadn't seen him in a very long time. He wanted you to meet him . . . But him and your mother fell out. They did that a lot,' he says. 'They liked each other, I'm sure. But things were difficult. They had no money and nowhere to go. And they had a row. A very silly row.'

'About what?'

'Boyd suggested she get some help. She had problems, Elvis, and she wasn't coping very well and she left with . . .' Lloyd slaps his hand over his mouth. 'Your father drove after her, but he'd been drinking and he swerved to avoid a rat and crashed into a tree.' Lloyd wipes his eyes. 'It was the worst night of my life.'

'What about my mum?'

Lloyd shakes his head. 'She thought you died too.'

'You should've told her!'

'I tried . . .' Lloyd pulls his hair. 'I had no name, no number. Nothing. I looked for her. Everywhere. But it was hopeless. Then she rang. Out of the blue.

I said, *Boyd's dead,* and she said, *Where's the baby?* and I said . . .

'What? What did you say?'

'He's gone.' Lloyd plasters back his hair. 'I didn't mean gone dead. I meant gone.'

'You left me on a bench!'

'I knew your father was finishing work. I knew the way he'd walk home. He always called in on Wednesdays – Janet used to pass on any hedgehogs from the area. He's great at rescuing things. Just think of all those hedgehogs, Elvis.'

'I'm not a hedgehog.'

'I knew he'd be wonderful!'

'Didn't you ring her back?'

'She hung up. She rang from a phone box. How could I trace her?'

'You had the address.' I think about the note.

'I found that in Boyd's notebook. So I copied it out. It was a guess. I thought. Well . . .'

'It was a clue?'

'Yes. And you'd have it for when you needed it. For when you needed to know.'

'We could've known loads sooner.'

'How? How could your dad come to Norway,

Elvis? He did it when you needed to know. When you wanted to find out, he gave up everything.'

I think about Dad's job.

I think about Lloyd standing up to Floyd just by being here.

'And Nina had her hands full with . . .'

'Nina?'

Lloyd looks up. I follow his eyes.

Sync

A silent dot pings out of the mist. It gets closer. And closer.

A white dinghy tacking towards us.

I see a girl with dark hair.

And a steel-set face.

Who pulls up alongside the *Gullfisk*.

I think about the dream.

The room I didn't know existed. A hand comes out of the mirror.

Lene.

It was Lene.

I look down.

Lene's dad was from England.

Lene's dad died when she was a baby.

Lene's mum has 'problems'.

She got the *Gullfisk* for her birthday.

In the summer.

Same as my birthday.

'Lene's mum is Nina,' I whisper out loud.

'She had her hands full with your sister ...'
Lloyd's voice trails off.

Me and Lene look at each other.

Lene holds her hand out like the dream.

It was her.

It was her face in the mirror.

I take it.

> 'You're my brother,'

> 'You're my sister,'

we say in sync.

Now

If you were looking down on Brymont on the 25th of June 2005, you'd have seen a man running, apples flying. Down Minton Street, past the Happy Shopper and the monkeys and the screech owls.

Writing:

HELP

and laying a baby down gently. Ever so gently on a bench and hiding by the lemurs.

Waiting for the Stetson to turn the corner . . .

And if you look down on the Traena Festival right now you'll see a woman tearing up papers and chucking them into the wind.

Three boats.

Together.

A dad in a blanket, a mum and an aunt on a bench.

A family like a jigsaw.

That makes it's own shape.
It's very own lovely wonky-edged imperfect shape.
With bits that stick out, rough and ready.
'Cos sometimes things don't slot together that
easy.

Twins

This is the story of what happened that night, the next day and twenty-five years before it.

The reason why I'm here now,

bobbing in a boat

with my mouth open,

part shock, part smile,

looking at a girl

who elbows me in the ribs and says, 'if you take the *Gullfisk* again, I'll kill you.' She looks at Lloyd. 'Tell him the rest,' she says and grins.

'Boyd was always Dad's favourite,' Lloyd says. 'Floyd hated that. When he died Mother swore us to secrecy, that we'd never tell Father. He had a heart condition. She thought it'd break his heart. So we kept it secret. He thought Boyd was off travelling the world.' He rubs the chrome railing. 'I made up postcards.'

I think about the brick through the window. 'He died and you and Floyd fell out.'

'Money,' Lloyd says. 'It all comes down to money.'

'Does Dad know?'

'Only the Boyd bit. Not the Floyd bit,' Lloyd says and puts his hands up. 'And he hasn't always known.'

I think back to the beginning, in the hedgehog basement. *George, can we discuss matters?* Dad's face when he came upstairs. 'You told him on my birthday?'

'Yes.' Lloyd sags like a leaky balloon.

'What about Lene?'

'No.' He shakes his head. 'I didn't tell a soul. I felt too ashamed.'

Lloyd looks up. 'Did she sign the papers?'

'No.' Lene laughs. 'She didn't. Thank God.' She tilts her head at the sun and grins. 'You still don't know do you? Tell him the good bit, Lloyd. Tell him the bit that changes everything.'

The Bit That Changes Everything

'Father died three years afterwards,' Lloyd says.

'After Boyd?'

He nods.

'Father had a lot of money.'

I think about the castle.

'And he left a lot of it to Boyd.'

'But Boyd was dead.'

Lloyd nods. 'Floyd thought the money would go to him as the eldest. But I told the estate manager he had children. Twins. None of them knew. Mother, Floyd, the estate. And now it's set to go to you. Both of you.'

'When we're thirteen.' Lene grins.

'I had to find you, Lene,' Lloyd says. 'I had to prove you existed. Floyd needed to prove you didn't. He used a private detective to find your mother. Before we came out here.'

'And one when we got here.' I tap my leg. 'To check we didn't get to her first.'

Lloyd nods.

'Floyd tried to get Mum to sign papers saying we weren't Boyd's. He came up here to make sure she did. To make sure she didn't get to meet you.' She elbows my arm and smiles. 'He offered her BIG money.' She bulges her eyes. 'But she didn't sign. She couldn't. She said we were the last piece of him she's got.'

'What's she like?'

She rolls her eyes. 'She isn't ... brilliant.'

I think about the phone call.

'That's why I go to Kirsten's.' She picks wood off the bottom of the boat. 'People come round to do "checks".'

'On what?'

'Food, money, stuff ... That I'm OK.'

'Why?'

'Sometimes I wasn't.' She shrugs. 'When I was little.'

'Can I see him?' I point at her chain. 'The photo.'

'Yeah.' Lene lifts the locket out of her shirt. 'Brother,' she says and laughs. 'That's mad.'

'I know.'

'It's brilliant though.'

And I unclick the locket and stare at the photo.

A Face

I look into his face.

Not really knowing what I'm looking for.

Just to see.

To see what I feel.

And I don't know yet.

Right now he's just a face.

Warm from Lene.

His hair is long. Tucked behind his ears.

He looks serious. And strange.

'Passport photo,' Lene says.

'Boyd hated having his photo taken,' Lloyd says.

I wonder if he's like me?

'Did Boyd get brain flicks, Lloyd?'

Lloyd nods. 'His brain was very flicky. He'd be halfway through a sandwich and decide to build a matchstick house.' He pulls his sleeves over his hands. 'The world was a bit of a cage for Boyd. It never really fitted him.'

Is he half of me?

One half?

The other one waiting on the island?

Are they halves or quarters?

I think about Dad. Always being there. Singing through it all.

Did he make me who I am?

I think about me.

Did I?

And Lloyd. And Aunty Ima.

I'm a collage.

I'm pieces of everyone and everything I've met.

Boyd isn't half.

He's just the beginning.

He's the seed.

Lloyd holds up his last Jazz apple. 'It was an apple tree,' he says. 'He crashed into an apple tree. I don't hold it against the apples. It isn't their fault.' He smooths its skin.

I think of how he plants a new tree in his orchard every year. 'It's how I remember him. When I'm with an apple, I'm with Boyd. People say the apple doesn't fall far from the tree. But it can. It can roll. It can roll all the way down the hill. I am a Partington. But I am nothing like Floyd. Boyd and I are our own people. He taught me to never forget that. So I don't.' He takes a bite.

I look down at the face.

It's good to see him.

It's kind of like a ghost though.

Something I can never touch.

I think of Dad, strong and real and always there.

And snap it shut.

Home

We look out at the mist which is pushing at the sides of the boat. Coming over the edges. And wrapping itself around us.

The boats chip the water and clunk noses.

'I don't want to be alarming –' Lloyd tries to paddle the mist away with his hands – 'but how are we going to get back?'

Lene looks over one shoulder then the other.

I hold up my dad's dad's dad's compass and swing it in my hand. 'With this!'

Lene grins and nods.

Bring us home, Great-Great-Great-Grandad, I think. *Take us home.*

The Unknown

We use the compass to guide us in. Lene shows me how.

I like the way the past is leading us to the future.

I think about me on my birthday.

Birthday me shrugs his shoulders at the me now.

There's so much I didn't know then. I'd never have guessed it.

From the island a foghorn blares. Pulling us in.

A lighthouse beam turns and flashes.

A glint of light in the white.

Sometimes you have to go out into the mist to discover things.

Sometimes it's when you jump into the unknown that you find out who you are.

How I See It

The boat pulls into the jetty.

The mist parts enough to see the shore.

I see Dad in a blanket.

I see Kirsten.

And a woman in between, not sure what to do with her hands. Running them over her hair. Tucking it behind her ears.

I don't know what to do either.

The festival goes on.

But the world goes silent.

For me.

For us?

I dunno.

'Elvis!' Lene yells. The *Gullfisk* bounces into the jetty.

CLUNK.

I snap out of it.

'Sorry.'

I switch the engine off.

My hands are shaking.

Lene climbs on to the jetty.

I chuck her the rope and she ties it up and hauls us in.

She leans over the boat and offers a hand.

I take it.

We look at each other.

Her eyes say she's got me. Whatever happens.

However this goes. Whatever it's like.

We've got each other.

I look at Mum.

Can I say that?

I can't even think it.

It's too weird.

I hold Lene's hand. My legs are wobbling. I feel like I'm gonna fall but I don't.

I pull myself up and out on to the shore.

She comes over to me.

Her.

The woman.

Mum.

For a long moment we just stare at each other.

It doesn't feel dreamy. And loving. And right.

It feels awkward.

And odd.

She puts her hand over her mouth and shakes her head like I'm not real.

'Hello,' I say.

'Hello,' she says and long wet trails run down both our faces.

Jessie Garon Presley

Elvis (Aaron) Presley had a twin who died before he
was born.

Jessie (Garon) Presley.

Maybe that gave Elvis a hole

that he could never fill.

Maybe he tried to cram it with stuff

to make the pain go away.

Or maybe he felt like a shadow,

like part of him was always missing.

I feel really sad for him

'cos Graceland mansion doesn't really mean
anything

if you rattle around hollow inside.

I think about Dad.

Maybe if Elvis had one person to hold on to

he wouldn't have needed to be important to
millions.

And that might have been enough

to stop him from dying on the toilet.

Alone.

Maybe.

I'm lucky.

I've got Lene.

And Dad.

And Lloyd and Aunty Ima and Bjorn and Mulki and Steinar and Jean.

We've got our invisible strings around us.

And my insides feel puffed up like a Jaffa Cake.

What If ...

What if it is the 25th of June 2018?

And in Brymont On Sea down Minton Street next to the Happy Shopper there is a shop. A new shop. And what if this shop is a community music shop – with a recording studio and free classes and posh coffee and guitar racks – called *Beats of the Streets*.

And what if there is a man with a trumpet (the new manager) and a boy with a triple-decker peanut-butter cake (the new owner) about to cut the opening ribbon, and a room full of people cheering and waving harmonicas and violins and bringing a bit of joy and possibility to the grey Brymont streets.

And what if there is a woman on an island with a pig that's just given birth to piglets, and rows of vegetables just sprouting, and lambs and strawberries that are being picked by Gunter from

Germany and Brian from Brazil, because she feels up for a new start.

And what if there's a girl and a boy and two men who are gonna be there that summer. And what if they spend all their summers there and learn how to sail. And Bjorn comes over and they all camp in the woods and make their own videos and don't care if people like them or not, 'cos who *actually* cares.

And what if George's great-great-grandad's ghost is proud.

And Boyd's ghost settles.

And Nina sells her story to the papers – FLOYD PARTINGTON TRIES TO DISINHERIT FAMILY – and Floyd loses his job and his power.

And Aunty Ima marries Mr Singh and his bees and moves down the road (now she doesn't have to help out with the rent).

And Lloyd builds an *Uncle's* cabin for Uncley times.

And Elvis sees his mum twice a year. Once in England. Once in Norway.

And they write emails, 'cos that feels easier.

And Lene comes over whenever she wants.

And has her own room.

And she can stay for as long as she likes . . .

What if?

What if?

What if?

Acknowledgements

This book happened thanks to a great many brilliant and beautiful people who I am very grateful to.

Firstly thanks to the wonderful Julia Darling Travel Fellowship award that enabled me to travel all over Norway meeting fantastic places and people and discovering all kinds of delicious things that this stunning country has to offer.

Julia Darling was a wonderful author, playwright and poet and very much loved and dearly missed. It was an honour to travel in her name. I tried to do it in as friendly and all encompassing way as possible to make the most of every last penny. THANK YOU! It was an unforgettable experience.

Thanks to the fab Faber team for their patience, support and loveliness and especially to my sage and broad-shouldered editor Alice Swan whose ever-calm and insightful brilliance was incredibly appreciated. You are truly a birth doula of books!

Thanks to the incredibly supportive and genuine

kinship of children's writers. I'm very chuffed to be part of you and our meet-ups make me very happy.

Thanks to all the writers who have gone before whose work inspires, delights and challenges me and to my friends and family and everyone out there I love, without whom I'd have been sunk many, many times.

In particular:

Chris, Tom, Wilf, Bob, Iorek and Twinks – Katie Darby-Villis, Pam Matthews, Penny Lee, Rachel Embleton and Debbie Lane – David Almond, Liz Flanagan, Brian Conaghan, Emma Carroll and Tove Jansson – Bev Robinson and Julia's family and friends – Claire Malcolm and New Writing North – the Hexham writing gang! – my big-hearted big sis Em, Mads and M&D.

Thanks for being there. I hope this crazy journey of a book makes you smile!

And lastly but very importantly ENORMOUS thanks to YOU the reader. Without you this story would never get the chance to come alive, which would make it very sad.

Thank YOU!

A talking mackerel changes everything ...

'This is the **real thing.**'
DAVID ALMOND

Fish Boy

Chloe Daykin

Loved this? Then try Chloe's astonishing debut:

People call me Fish Boy.
My skin goes up and down like the waves.
My mind goes in and out like the sea.

Billy's got a lot on his mind – that he'd rather not think or talk about. So he watches David Attenborough and swims in the sea, letting his mind drift.

Then Patrick Green arrives with 'fingers like steel, strength of a bear' and a talking mackerel swims up to Billy's face.

The adventure begins . . .

With illustrations by Richard Jones.

WINNER – NORTHERN WRITERS AWARD
SHORTLISTED – BRANFORD BOASE AWARD
LONGLISTED – UKLA BOOK AWARDS